The Full Circle Ranch Saga

The Locket's Secret

Book 1

ELIZABETH JEAN THOMAS

Cover by Elizabeth Jean Thomas

ISBN 979-8-89130-700-1 (paperback)
ISBN 979-8-89130-701-8 (digital)

Christian Faith Publishing
832 Park Avenue
Meadville, PA 16335
www.christianfaithpublishing.com

Printed in the United States of America

TABLE OF CONTENTS

CHAPTER 1
Daniel

"Come on, Daniel. You can take him!" Someone shouted as a teenage boy was thrown back against the wall.

Throwing a punch, the boy sent the approaching fighter stumbling back.

From the other side of the street, someone cried, "Come on, Josh! Show him who's boss!"

As the boy called Josh caught his footing, the one who had been called Daniel studied his opponent. The boy was bigger than he was, but that was his misfortune. Standing at only five foot two, Daniel was used to dealing with those bigger than him.

Josh put up a valiant effort but was no match against the lightning speed and thundering blows, which suddenly came from his opponent. Quickly his feet were swept out from under him, and Josh found himself lying flat on his back.

Scrambling up to his knees, he threw up his hands. "No!" he cried. "I give!"

Getting to his feet, Josh faced the other fighter. "Where'd you learn to fight like that?" He asked. He was half amazed and half angry that the smaller boy had beaten him.

The smaller boy didn't answer but instead offered his hand silently. Josh stared at it for a moment, then accepted it.

As Daniel and his companion left, Daniel reached into the pocket of his coat. "You know," he said, retrieving an old pocketknife. "Josh said, 'I give,' and give he did."

He tossed the knife to his friend. "See what you can get for it. We'll meet up tomorrow in the usual place."

With that, the two boys parted ways.

The next day also found Daniel in a fight. This time, he stood across from the boy who, just yesterday, had been a friend.

"You shouldn't have tried to steal from me, Michael." Daniel said.

Michael Young took a fighting stance, saying, "Oh, come on, Daniel. Don't ever trust a thief. You taught me that yourself."

With that thought, he delivered a stunning blow, which knocked Daniel back against the wall. It also knocked the cap Daniel always wore to the ground, allowing a long, dark braid to fall down her back.

The approaching boy stopped midswing, and his eyes widened in shock. "D-Daniel? Y-you're a girl?"

The teenage girl, who now stood before him, took advantage of her opponent's surprise. Before he could recover, she charged and took him down.

Looking down at him, she said, "Looks like I didn't teach you everything I know." Leaning down, she grabbed the bag from the boy's belt and shook out the money. Taking half of it, she spoke, "I should be taking more for my trouble. Don't ever try to steal from me again, Michael."

With that, she left him there, staring after her. Making her way to the saloon, she walked through the swinging doors. As soon as she did, her nose was assaulted by the familiar smell of whiskey.

As she entered, the bartender looked up and saw her. "Daniel, what are you doin' here, lass? Yer shift doesn't start for nigh an hour," he said in his clipped Irish accent.

Walking up to the bar, she smiled at her good friend. "My other work ended early," she said.

He glanced up from the drink he was pouring and saw a large bruise starting to appear on the side of her face. "Come into the backroom, lass. I'll be having a look at that."

Daniel tried to protest, but the man insisted. Soon they were in the bartender's office, and the Irishman was dabbing at the bloody cut on her forehead.

"Aye, it's a grand one you've got. Ye ought not to be fightin', lass," he scolded.

Daniel smiled up at him. "Says the man who's been known to throw people out those very swinging doors on more than one occasion."

Returning her smile, he set aside the cloth he had been using. Then he sat back on the edge of the desk. "That is what I like about ye, Daniel. We're alike in so many ways."

Changing the subject, he said, "Since ye be here so early, I reckon there wasn't many takers."

Daniel shook her head. "No. Today was a battle between me and that low-down, thieving skunk of a partner of mine. After a girl beat his britches off, he wasn't so eager to try again."

Marely O'Brian threw his head back and laughed. He could imagine the surprise the boy must have felt upon discovering that Daniel was, in fact, a girl. He himself had mistaken the young teenager for a boy when they had first met.

Daniel had come in wearing old ill-fitting trail clothes and a coonskin cap, which had come down to hide part of her dirt-streaked face. Her hair had been tied back in a braid and hidden up beneath the hat. It had not been until she had spoken to him, several days after their first meeting, that her voice revealed that she was, in fact, a young girl.

When she had asked about a job, Marely had been tempted to say no because she was so young. But the girl had amused him, and he had liked her from the moment he laid eyes on her. So he offered her the job, despite her young age, hoping to protect her from having to work in the rougher saloons that plagued the town.

Therefore, he had hired her. He made sure her dresses were more modest than the older women's and kept a watchful eye over her. Daniel was his favorite, and more than once, he told her that she was like his own daughter, who died before he left Ireland in 1850.

The other girls liked Daniel too. This was because that even though she was young, if any of the customers gave them a hard time, Daniel could usually talk them out of the situation.

Soon, it was time for her shift to begin. Marely headed back out front while Daniel changed into her working outfit. This Saturday night, she stayed extremely busy, passing out drinks and talking to the customers. Unfortunately, the night was not going to end as well as it had begun.

Her shift had just ended when a cry rang through The Lucky Shamrock. Turning from the bar, Daniel saw Crystal, the girl closest to her own age, holding a hand to her tear-streaked face. Her other arm was locked in the grip of a young man who wasn't much older than his prisoner.

Without even hesitating, Daniel walked over and stepped between Crystal and the customer. Talking to him, she managed to pull his attention from the weeping girl. One of the other women came and led Crystal away.

Daniel managed to get the man up from the table and walked him to the door. As they headed that way, the drunken trailhand stumbled, and the rest of the crowd laughed.

As he regained his footing, Daniel slipped her hand inside his pocket and retrieved a watch. Hiding it away in her hand, she got the man out the door and turned back to Crystal. The girl thanked her and insisted that she was not seriously hurt.

At that moment, Marely came from the storage room, and she saw the three girls standing together by the bar. Daniel told him about the man who had struck Crystal.

"Do you want me to finish your shift?" Daniel offered.

Crystal shook her head. "No, I really need this job." She choked back a stuttered sob.

"Ye needn't be worryin' about yer job, lass," Marely assured her. "Take the rest o' the night off. One of the other lasses will cover for ye, I'm sure."

Daniel nodded at his words. "I already said I would," she pointed out. Another tear escaped Crystal's eye, and she said, "Thank you, D-Daniel." She reached out and hugged her friend.

Awkwardly, Daniel returned her hug. She wasn't comfortable with people thanking her. "Go get changed and head on home," she said.

Crystal had just left to change when the doors slammed open.

"Where is she?" someone bellowed.

Everyone looked up to see the drunken young man Daniel had just rescued Crystal from. Looking around, he spotted the "she" he was looking for and drunkenly stormed toward Daniel.

"Try to make a fool out of me, will you?" he snarled.

Marely stepped between the two, but the man was so angry that he grabbed the Irishman and thew him aside like a sack of potatoes.

Grabbing Daniel by the arm, he shouted, "Give it back to me, you little wench! Before I beat it out of you!"

"What are you talking about?" Daniel asked, carefully slipping the man's watch back in his pocket.

Shaking her, the man growled again, "You stole my watch! Now give it back!"

Daniel protested that she didn't have it. When the man discovered it was in his pocket, he grew even angrier.

Even as drunk as he appeared to be, he was still able to deliver a punch that sent the girl clear across the room. She slammed into the bar and felt something snap. She lay there, unable to move, barely able to breathe.

The man stalked toward her but suddenly stopped. He tensed for just a moment before sprawling headlong into one of the empty tables.

"Never let it be said that Marely O'Brian's girls can't take care of themselves." Daniel looked up to see Crystal standing there, holding a broken bottle in her hand.

Daniel smiled up at her and tried to laugh. Instantly, however, the attempt turned into a moan. Quickly she wrapped her arm around her chest and closed her eyes.

Hurrying over to her, Marely called out, "Everybody out! We're closing early."

As the men walked and staggered out the door, Marely gave a new order. "One of ye run and fetch the doctor!"

When the doctor arrived, he took one look at the teenager and had her taken to a backroom. There, he examined her and found that one of her ribs had been broken. When he was done, having wrapped it tightly, he went out to where the bartender was waiting.

"How bad is she?" Marely asked, his hands nervously wringing in front of him.

The doctor looked up at him. "She has a broken rib. The girl's lucky it didn't puncture a lung. Crystal is in with her now, trying to get her to rest."

"Can she ride?" Marley asked.

The doctor glanced at him suspiciously. "I wouldn't suggest it." Then he quickly added, "Why do you ask?"

"Because one o' the lasses who works for me brought word. The man who did this, he is plannin' on coming back after 'er. He might just kill her this time and anyone who gets in his way," Marely replied.

The doctor was startled. "But she's just a child!" he exclaimed.

"This fellow doesn't care. He said if she be old enough to work in a saloon…" Marely didn't finish the thought. Sighing, he continued, "I hired the lass so she wouldn't go to the other saloons."

The doctor put a hand on the bartender's shoulder. "I know what the girl means to you. With time and rest, she should heal nicely."

Suddenly Crystal burst out of the back room. "She's gone! I turned around for a minute, and when I turned back, she was gone!"

In an effort to calm the girl, Marely put his hands on her shoulders. "Take a breath, lass. Now tell me what's wrong?" he said.

Following his advice, Crystal took a shaky breath. "It's Daniel. She's gone. She seemed to be in a lot of pain, so I turned to get her some of the stuff the doctor left. When I turned back to give it to her, she was gone!"

The doctor glanced at the girl, surprised. "I gave her something for the pain before coming out here. It should have kept her resting for at least another two hours."

The bartender moved past them and entered the room. He walked over to the table and glanced down at the cup that sat on a table. "Ye may have given it to her doctor. But she didn't take it."

He walked over to the window, which was now open, and looked out into the inky darkness. "And wherever she be, she's long gone now."

As soon as Daniel had heard that someone was after her, she had taken off. She hadn't waited to say goodbye to the man who had treated her like his daughter. Nor had she said goodbye to Crystal either.

She knew that if she waited to do so, they would try to help her. But they couldn't. They would only slow her down, possibly getting hurt, or worse, in the process.

Daniel knew the land that lay around the town like the back of her hand. It was her home. Nobody in town knew that she didn't live in a real house, not even Marely.

All they knew was that one day, an orphan girl had showed up and turned the town on its head. Within the first few days, she had been pulled into the world of thieves, had gotten a job at The Lucky Shamrock, and had even gotten arrested.

The people in town soon became used to Daniel's rough ways. But nobody knew anything about her. And that was the way Daniel liked it.

Now as she headed out of town, she swung by the cave that she had built into a home. There she stuffed her few belongings into the threadbare bag, which had been sitting next to the wall.

Into the sack, she put a knife, several books of matches, a half-burned candle, and a locket. She also added a bit of food she had purchased.

Stepping to the edge of the cave, she gave a whistle and waited. A moment later, out of the bushes appeared a beautiful black-and-white stallion.

"Wonderer," she greeted the horse, "we have to go."

The horse snorted and moved his head as if to say, "Of course, let's get going."

Though she had no saddle, having sold it long ago, the girl mounted the animal easily. Then with rider and animal as one, they turned and vanished into the growing darkness.

Leaving her past behind her, she traveled for three and a half weeks, mainly headed West. It was on the beginning of the fourth week that she rode into a new town. For some reason, as she hitched her horse to the rail, the town gave her a strange feeling, almost as if she had been there before.

A quick search of the town revealed it to be larger than the one she previously resided in. This town seemed to have a population of seven hundred people.

Deciding to stay, she once again mounted the animal and rode two miles to the south. There, she found an abandoned shack. It appeared as though nobody had used it for years, so Daniel decided to make it her new home.

Marely had paid her well. But even with the money she had made with Michael, she had only been able to purchase supplies for her and her mount, leaving little more than two dollars in her pocket.

As she dismounted, the movement sent pain shooting through her. She had been set back in the healing process when her stallion had stumbled during a storm. There had been no chance of her staying mounted, and she hit the ground hard, thus adding further damage to the already-injured bones. She was painfully reminded of the incident as her feet hit the ground.

Examining the shack, she thought about fixing it up. But night was falling, and she thought it best to wait until the morning, perhaps even until she had healed some more. So she watered her horse in the nearby stream and returned to the shack to bed down for the night.

As the sun was rising the next morning, Daniel left her new home and headed into town. Before the day was up, she knew the town inside and out. She managed to find a job in the saloon and had even made friends with the general store owner, a Mr. Brown.

The last place she explored was the cemetery, which rested atop a hill. From the highest point on the hill, hidden in the shadow of a large tombstone, she watched the town, which was now alive with people. Standing there, watching the goings-on, she thought that perhaps one day, she could call this place home.

CHAPTER 2
Maria

It was an unusually warm fall day on the Full Circle Ranch. The owner of the ranch, a fourteen-year-old girl by the name of Maria Jackson, watched as her foreman worked to break a horse. As she watched him, she joined the other hired hands, who cheered for the man on horseback.

A few moments later, the man was thrown from the horse and hit the ground violently. As he scrambled away from the jumping, snorting animal, Maria rushed toward him. "Mr. Thompson! Are you alright?"

The foreman glanced down at her and finished dusting himself off. Pushing his hat back on his head, he replied, "I'm alright, Maria. That horse didn't throw me hard enough to do anything besides get me all dirty."

Maria smiled. "I'm glad, Mr. Thompson."

Now that the horse was standing still, the two walked over to it. She tried to shy away from them, but being tied as it was, she couldn't go far.

Gently Maria reached out and petted the horse's nose. "It's alright, Buttercup. Easy, girl," she said softly.

Glancing up at Mr. Thompson, Maria saw him smiling. "What's so funny?" she asked.

11

"You've got your father's natural way with horses," he explained.

"I'm glad Papa asked you to be my legal guardian, Mr. Thompson," Maria said.

The foreman, who had been her father's best friend, smiled down at Maria. "I am too," he said, remembering the day Maria's father had come to him and expressed his concern.

He and Jackson had just witnessed the hanging of Brent Mitchell, a horse thief and murderer. On the way back to his office, Jackson had been quiet. Finally, he had invited Thompson in for coffee.

Accepting the offer, Thompson had sat with Jackson in the office for several moments before the sheriff finally spoke.

"You know something, John?" he had asked. "Being a sheriff makes you realize just how fragile life is."

John Thompson had been unable to answer that. But apparently his friend didn't expect one because he continued, "I met Mitchell's family yesterday. He has a wife and a daughter no older than Maria." For a long moment, the sheriff fell silent again. Then he continued, "John, I'm going to ask you a favor. It's important, but I'll understand if you want to refuse." Then he went on to explain the favor.

At first, the foreman couldn't believe what his best friend was asking him to do. But once the shock wore off, he accepted the honor wholeheartedly.

Once he agreed, some of the tension and worry left the sheriff's eyes. "Thank you, John. I feel better knowing that if something should happen to both Caroline and me, Maria would be taken care of."

Walking the horse back to the barn, Thompson was suddenly pulled back to the present when Maria noticed one of the new hands—a boy, perhaps a year older than Maria herself.

"How's the new hand doing?" she asked.

The foreman glanced over to where the boy was working on shoeing a horse. "Thomas is doing right fine," Mr. Thompson stated.

Maria smiled. "I'm glad to hear it. I know you were worried about hiring him on."

The foreman nodded. "He didn't seem to know much about horses when he showed up. But he's a quick learner."

Once they reached the barn, the two brushed down the horse, as well as fed and watered her. When she was ready for the night, the foreman left to tend to his other duties, and Maria finished caring for the rest of the stabled horses.

Supper was always a family affair. These men were the only family Maria had in the world, and she treated them as such. Every night, the men would wash up after work and then join Maria in the house for supper and conversation.

Then sometimes, depending on the night, Thomas would stay and help her clean up. Tonight was one of those nights. As they washed dishes, they discussed the ranch.

It surprised her that while Thomas didn't know much about raising horses, he had a wide knowledge of the land. He presented many good and interesting ideas on how to produce a better crop.

Maria asked him how he knew so much about the land, and he smiled.

Then he explained by saying, "My father was a farmer. He loved the land."

Soon they were done. Thomas excused himself and bid Maria a good night. Then he headed out to the bunkhouse. Taking one last look around the kitchen, Maria went to bed.

The next morning, she rose early and got her share of the work done. Once she was finished with her morning chores, she hitched the wagon and drove into town.

The first place she stopped was the leather shop. Parking the wagon, she entered the shop. Over at the workbench, a man sat fixing a leather strap. When Maria entered, he looked up and greeted her. "Hello, Maria."

"Morning, Mr. Mason," Maria returned. "I came by to check on that saddle I brought in last week."

Paul Mason stood and said, "Just got finished with it last night." He informed her with a smile. He retrieved the saddle and set it up on the counter. "Was going to bring it out later today."

Maria returned his smile. "Well, now you don't have to make that long trip." Looking over the saddle, she added, "Your work is amazing, as always."

Mr. Mason smiled. "Why, thank you, Maria. Means a lot to a fellow to know his work is appreciated."

Maria handed him the agreed-upon price. Then she said, "Would you mind putting it in my wagon, Mr. Mason?"

Mr. Mason smiled at the girl. "Of course not, Maria. Don't worry about it."

With a thank-you, she left and headed to the general store. Behind the counter, a man in his late fifties stood, taking stock of his shelves.

Glancing up, he said, "Well, hello, Maria. What can I do for you today?"

Walking up to the counter, Maria smiled at the man who had been a close friend throughout her entire life. "Hello, Mr. Brown," she replied. "I was just needing some things for the ranch."

She handed him the list, and he read over it.

"I'll get these things for you," he said.

Thanking him, Maria turned to look at the shelves of items he had in his store. "Mr. Brown, you always have the nicest store in town," Maria stated.

Packing away the last of her items in a box, Mr. Brown spoke, "Why, thank you, Maria." When she pulled a few bills out, he shook his head. "Don't worry about that today, Maria. I'll just put it on your bill, and we'll settle at the end of the month like always."

Putting away her money, Maria retrieved her boxes. "Thank you, Mr. Brown," she said. "I'd best be getting back to the ranch."

When she arrived at the ranch, Thomas came and helped her unload the wagon. She handed him the saddle, which he put into the tack room. When he returned, he retrieved the last crate from the wagon and took it into Maria, who thanked him.

When he turned to go, Maria stopped him. "Hold up a moment, Thomas. Do you have time to talk?"

Turning back to her, he asked, "About what?"

Maria motioned to the kitchen table and said, "I was wanting to hear more about the idea you had for improving the hay crop."

Surprised, Thomas smiled. "You mean crop rotation?"

Sitting, Maria nodded. "Yes, what does that mean?"

Taking a chair across from her, Thomas began explaining. "Every year you've been planting hay, or rather alfalfa, in the same fields. But if you rotate your crops, it means that instead of planting hay next year in those same fields, you plant something else, like corn for example. This gives the earth time to heal from caring for the hay while still producing a crop you can use."

Maria nodded understandingly. However, she said, "But we feed the horses with the hay."

"True," Thomas agreed. He glanced out the window and said, "But you have a lot of land here, Maria—more than your largest heard needs. You might consider using more of it for planting. Use the newly planted ground for hay and the old for corn. Then the following year, you can switch it."

Maria seemed to think for a moment. "It sounds like a good plan. I'd like to talk it over with Mr. Thompson and see what he thinks." Standing, she said, "Go find Mr. Thompson and ask him to meet us at the South Range." With that, she ran toward the barn and began saddling her horse.

About fifteen minutes later, Thomas and Mr. Thompson rode up beside her. When they reached her, Mr. Thompson said, "Thomas said you wanted to discuss something?"

Maria nodded. "Yes, as you know, we didn't have a good alfalfa crop this past year. Thomas had an idea of how to do better next year." Turning to Thomas, she asked him to explain.

Thomas once again explained the idea of crop rotation. While he was speaking, Maria watched the foreman closely. When Thomas finished, Mr. Thompson said nothing.

Impatient to hear his answer, Maria questioned, "What do you think, Mr. Thompson?"

Still, the foreman remained quiet.

Finally, he spoke, "I don't know much about crops. I've been a horseman all my life. But I don't see any reason it shouldn't work."

At Maria's encouragement, Thomas went on to explain that the best time to plow was a few weeks before planting. However, they decided it would be best to break the ground open before the cold weather settled in.

Since Thomas had the most experience with farming, it was decided he would oversee this project. In the weeks that followed, he worked hard. And by the time the cold weather settled in, the right amount of earth had been broken open.

About a week later, Maria and most of the men went into town. She sternly reminded, as she always did, not to get drunk, and as always, they promised her they would not.

Then while they went to play a few games of poker, she went to visit with Mr. Brown.

As soon as she entered the general store, he greeted her. Soon they were sitting in the back, drinking a cup of hot chocolate. While they were enjoying the warmth the drink provided, Mr. Brown asked, "So the ranch is doing well?"

"Yes, sir," Maria replied. "We've been doing very well. I'm sure the horses will please the racers. In fact, we almost have another broken in."

Peter Brown knew that Maria and her hands trained horses not only for the Calvary but to race. Every year, during the spring race, she would bring some of her horses to either rent or sell. Sometimes she would sell one; other times, she wouldn't. Either way was alright because Maria herself joined in the race and had fun.

They talked for a while, and then Maria said, "Well, I want to go and talk to the sheriff."

"The sheriff?" Mr. Brown asked, alarmed. "Has there been any trouble?"

Maria was quick to assure him that this was not the case. "No," she said, "I just wanted to say hello to a family friend."

Having assured him that everything was alright, she left and crossed the street to the jail.

"Maria, how are you today?" Sheriff Johnson asked.

"Good. How are you, Sheriff?" she returned.

"Fine," the sheriff answered. "Things have been pretty quiet since the reverend left."

Maria laughed. "What was he in for this time?" she asked.

The sheriff shook his head. "Same thing as usual. I told him he ought to keep his preaching in the church and out of the saloon. And do you know what he told me?"

Still laughing, Maria shook her head. "No, but I can probably guess."

The sheriff nodded. "Yes, you probably could. Something about if sinners won't come to him, he'd go to the sinners."

They both laughed, and the sheriff took a drink of his coffee. "Like I said, it's been pretty quiet since he left. Only got one new prisoner."

Now Maria glanced at him curiously. "Oh?" she asked.

Again, the sheriff nodded. "A young one too. She's nothing but a kid really—a year or two younger than yourself I'd say."

Maria's curious expression turned to one of surprise. "She? The prisoner is a girl? What did she do?"

The sheriff shook his head. "Nothing too serious—yet. Just got into fights mostly. Though she did have one charge of theft pressed against her. But the man dropped it when she returned what she took. She'll be released tomorrow."

Maria nodded. "Well, perhaps it will teach her something."

Sheriff Johnson glanced at the door, which separated the cells from the office area. "I doubt it. Those types don't learn very fast. Most of them grow up to become outlaws and wind up dead—either by being shot or swingin' on the gallows."

Suddenly the sheriff realized how young the girl sitting before him really was. Quickly he changed the subject.

Soon, they heard a sound from the other side of the door. Walking over, Maria looked through the little window. From there, she could see a girl curled up in the cell on the right.

Maria was somewhat disappointed. The girl was turned away from her, and from Maria's current position, she wasn't able to see anything except that the girl had long dark-brown hair that had gone uncut for a long time.

Turning back to the sheriff, she glanced outside and realized evening had come. She said goodbye and went to gather her men. Then they all headed back to do their evening ranch chores. During that time, Maria's mind stayed on the girl sitting in the sheriff's jail.

That night was spent tossing and turning. Suddenly Maria bolted upright, startled out of a horrible nightmare.

Catching her breath, she closed her eyes. When she did, images from the nightmare appeared in her mind—the images of a faceless girl, whose body swung from wooden gallows.

CHAPTER 3
Samantha

"Samantha! You cannot be seriously considering staying in this uncivilized town!" a young woman exclaimed, drawing her cloak around her.

"Jenifer!" her friend protested. "We came out West to have an adventure. What better place than a little frontier town?"

"It's uncivilized." Jenifer sniffed. "If you wanted an adventure, why couldn't you find one in Boston?" she complained as she stepped directly into a mud puddle.

Samantha laughed at the disgusted expression on her friend's face as the young woman examined the now-muddy skirt. "Please, Samantha, get your adventure over quickly so we can return to Boston where we belong."

"Oh, Jenifer!" Samantha said, taking her friend by the arm. "When I suggested this trip, you said it was exciting."

"I said it *sounded* exciting—like something out of those books you are always reading. I told Father he should never have let you purchase those. And I never said I wanted to conduct an adventure of my own," Jenifer corrected.

"Then why did you agree to accompany me?" Samantha questioned.

"Simply to make sure you stayed out of trouble until you returned home," Jenifer replied.

With that, the conversation ended as the two young women made their way down the sidewalk.

They spent the next several hours looking through the stores and shops that lined Main Street. The amount of time it took for these girls to look in so few places surprised the storekeepers. Finally, evening came, and they headed to the hotel.

As they walked, they noticed the sheriff making his rounds, and the two parties met.

"Hello, Marshal," Jenifer greeted the lawman.

The sheriff smiled and tipped his hat. "Well, I'm not a Marshal, just the sheriff of Larson, Miss…" His voice trailed off questioningly.

"Jenifer Stone," the young woman offered.

"Miss Stone and Miss…"

Samantha took his offered hand. "Samantha Kincaid," she replied.

The sheriff nodded politely. "Miss Stone and Miss Kincaid, I must say it was a pleasure to meet you." A moment later, he added, "Now I don't want to frighten you young ladies, but I suggest you retire to the hotel. Normally, Larson's a peaceful town, but it never hurts to be careful."

Jenifer smiled at the lawman. "Oh, of course, Sheriff. We were on our way there now. Thank you for the warning. It is very much appreciated."

With that, the two girls headed for the hotel.

Within the next few days, nothing really happened. Jenifer grew bored with the little town and boarded the train back East. As they awaited its arrival, Jenifer desperately tried once more to get her friend to return with her.

"Samantha, why? Why do you want to stay here?" she asked. "There is nothing here for you."

At these words, Samantha's smile faded. "I…I don't feel that way Jenny. It feels more like…well…like I am supposed to be here."

Jenifer shook her head. "Well, I certainly don't feel that way. I am returning home. You will come back too. You'll see."

They said goodbye, and Jenifer boarded the train. Samantha waited until she could no longer see her friend waving to her. Then she turned, wondering if she had made a mistake. But she shook off the feeling and returned to the hotel.

After returning to her room, she retrieved a book from her suitcase. She then took it outside and walked to the small park, which she had been both surprised and pleased to discover the day she had arrived.

A few hours later, it became surprisingly hot, and she found herself in need of something to drink. As much as she hated to, she wandered into the saloon as the hotel's dining room was closed for maintenance—something about a fire.

As she entered the saloon, she smiled, remembering how the fire had started. She and Jenifer had sat down for supper one night when an elderly man smoking a cigar had come in.

As the man made his way into the dining room, he was run into by a rowdier customer, causing him to bump into the girls' table and drop his cigar right onto Jenifer's lap.

The frightened young woman had thrown the cigar onto the table, where it set the tablecloth aflame. In an effort to put out the flames, the man who dropped the cigar threw the cloth onto the floor. Unfortunately, the flames only grew until Samantha thought the entire hotel was going to burn.

Thankfully, the manager of the hotel had been able to put out the flames. Unfortunately, however, by that time, the fire had caught ahold of other tables and the curtains. In the end, the dining room had been destroyed, which is why Samantha was forced to enter the saloon for a drink, seeing as there was no parlor or anyplace a young lady would go.

As she entered the structure, she thought of her friend. Jenifer would be horrified that Samantha had even considered going into a place like this.

Making her way over to the bar, she caught the attention of the bartender, who cleared his throat. "Sorry, miss," he said gruffly. "I don't serve ladies. Besides, you don't look old enough to drink."

Samantha smiled at him. "That's alright. Even if I were old enough, I wouldn't drink alcohol. I was hoping, however, that I might trouble you for some lemonade." She told the story of the hotel fire.

Laughing at her tale, the bartender poured her a glass of lemonade. She thanked him and was about to pay for it when he said, "On the house, miss."

Thanking him again, she turned and looked around. She blushed at the sight of women in their bright-colored short-skirted dresses. The only things that covered their legs from the knee down were tights and garters.

Therefore, she turned her attention to the piano player. For a while, she listened to him, thinking that he was doing a very good job.

Having finished her lemonade, she placed the glass on the bar and started to leave. However, she was suddenly grabbed from behind.

"Hey now, little missy, come have a drink and dance with me," a young man, a boy really, said.

"Let go of me!" Samantha demanded. She tried to pull away, but his grip was too strong.

Samantha would never be able to explain what happened. One minute, he was standing there, trying to steer her farther into the saloon; the next minute, he was holding a hand to his cheek with blood running from a cut.

After that incident, she returned to the hotel. Samantha was shaken from her experience in the saloon. Though she had longed for adventure and excitement, that was not what she had in mind. It was almost enough to convince her to return to Boston. But stubbornly she pushed that thought aside.

Soon, it had been a week since her friend left, but other than the one incident, Samantha was having the time of her life. "I can't believe Jenifer didn't want to stay," she said to herself one morning.

The morning was Sunday, and she had been happy to discover that the little town had a church. As she headed to the building, which sat at the edge of town, she was glad to see many people there.

They entered and soon began to sing, beginning with her favorite: "Amazing Grace." Soon they moved on to the seasonal carols such as "Joy to the World," "Silent Night," and her favorite "Away in a Manger."

As she sang, she glanced around. She noticed a couple of ragged-looking teenagers, some her own age but some younger, standing and sitting in a corner.

As she studied the group, she noticed one, who seemed to love the songs as much as she did.

Then came the message. Samantha was spellbound by the reverend's enchanting voice. She had been to church her entire life, but never had she heard such a simple and heartfelt presentation of the Gospel.

After the service ended, she thought of the child she had noticed earlier. She looked for the girl but couldn't find her. Giving up, she returned to the hotel and wrote to her friend.

Sitting at the small table in her room, she thought for several moments, then began her letter.

December 1885

Dear Jenifer,

I can't believe it has already been a week since you left. During that time, I've seen and experienced so much that it seems like we only arrived yesterday.

Everyone here is nice. I think they are ready for the Christmas holidays. Mr. Brown, the general store owner, has set a large nativity scene in his store window. He said that his grandfather hand-carved the pieces and let him help with the animals. He also said that's why the sheep look more like buffalo.

I know you'll be absolutely horrified when I tell you what I did last week. Do you remember the fire in the hotel dining room? Well, it is taking longer than expected to repair the damage.

As you know, the hotel is the only decent place to get a meal and something to drink. Therefore, I was left with no choice but to enter the Desert Flower.

I wish I could see your expression as you read that statement. I'm sure you recall the Desert Flower is the name of the local saloon.

Even though I write about this expe-rience humorously, I must admit that I was left a bit shaken by it. As I was preparing to leave the Desert Flower, a young man, a year older than myself I would guess, grabbed me. He said he wanted us to drink and dance together.

I fought against him, but even though he was well on his way to being drunk, his grip was strong. I couldn't get away, and he would have gotten what he wanted, except someone smashed a bottle and cut his face with the jagged end.

Whoever it was that rescued me has my eternal gratitude. I am only sorry that I did not see who it was so I could thank him.

On a lighter note, let me tell you about the church service I attended this morning. I wish you could have been here for it. The service was nothing like what we have attended in Boston.

While hundreds of people attend any given church, here only a handful of people attend. But that somehow seems fitting. The songs are powerful, and the service a simple one—simple yet moving.

I close this letter by wishing you a Merry Christmas, a Happy New Year as well.

Your friend,
Samantha

After signing the letter, she sealed it in an envelope. Then she walked it down to the manager and asked him to send it. Then she left the hotel and walked around town until it grew dark.

She wanted to see if she could find the girl she had seen in church. For some reason, she couldn't get the image of the girl from her mind. But the teenagers were nowhere to be found.

As she turned to go back to the hotel, she suddenly felt a hand on her shoulder. Surprised, she spun around and cried out. "Oh! Sheriff!" she exclaimed. "You startled me."

Smiling down at the young woman, he apologized, "I'm sorry, Miss Kincaid. I saw you walking alone and wanted to warn you. This is the shadier side of town and is no place for a young lady, especially after dark."

Samantha returned his smile. "No harm done," she said. "Thank you, Sheriff, and please, call me Samantha."

"Alright, then, Samantha," he said with a smile. "Would you mind if an old sheriff escorted you back to the hotel?" he asked. His eyes sparkled as he offered her his arm.

"That would be most kind of you, Sheriff," Samantha replied with a smile. She took his arm.

They headed back to the hotel, and there they said good night. As Samantha changed into her nightgown, her mind stayed on the girl she had seen at church.

Her last thought as she fell asleep was *tomorrow, I will find that child.* But in the morning, the stranger was completely forgotten.

C H A P T E R 4
The Meeting

The cold weather that usually came in December finally settled in. Maria was in town purchasing supplies for the ranch. She was tired of riding, and it was several miles back to the ranch. So she decided to walk to the small park at the edge of town.

For as long as she could remember, the park had been there. People said it began as a simple playground for the children of the town's founder. It then grew as the years passed, and more people settled in.

To her surprise, she saw a girl she had never seen before. Walking over, she greeted the stranger, "Hello, my name is Maria."

The girl glanced up from her book to see a girl younger than herself. "Hello," she returned, "I am Samantha."

Placing the book in her handbag, Samantha rose. As she did, she heard the other girl say "I don't believe I've seen you in town before."

Facing Maria, Samantha smiled. "I'm still new here. I've only been in town for a month."

As they spoke, they began walking down the streets. They were passing by an alley when Samantha smelled something awful. "Oh, goodness. What is that?" she asked, grimacing.

"What?" Maria asked, turning to her new friend.

Samantha shook her head. "That awful odor. Can't you smell it?"

Glancing around quickly, Maria shook her head. "No, but I'm pretty much immune to most smells. I do live on a ranch."

They were about to move on, but the younger girl stopped short when she caught a movement out of the corner of her eye. "What in the world?" she asked.

Maria stepped into the shadows and found herself looking at a girl who sat digging among the trash someone had thrown out. The girl was filthy from head to toe.

"Hello," Maria stated softly.

At first, the girl just stared at them. It seemed like she didn't know whether to stay put and fight or to run.

"It's okay. You can come on out. We're not going to hurt you," Maria said. Then she introduced herself. "I'm Maria by the way."

Slowly the girl came out to the sidewalk, and Maria moved to stand beside her. For a long moment, she continued studying the two older girls and finally offered a hand. "Daniel." That was all she said.

The two older girls studied Daniel in return. Finally, Samantha asked, "Who are your parents? *Where* are they?"

Sorrow came into the girl's dark eyes. At last, she said, "They're dead." Her tone was hard but still full of sadness.

Maria wanted to reach out and embrace the girl, but she wasn't sure how she would react. So instead, she said, "I'm sorry. My parents are dead too. They died in a fire. My pa was sheriff and he captured a gang leader. The men in the gang burned down our barn with my parents trapped inside."

Samantha nodded. "Mine have passed away as well. Their death was due to a carriage accident. The driver had been drinking without my parents' knowledge. They told him to slow down, but he kept going faster. When he made a sharp turn, another carriage happened to be coming, and the two collided. I was thrown out during the turn, and it saved my life. My parents were not so lucky."

Turning to the youngest girl, Maria spoke. "How did you parents die?" she asked.

Without even blinking, the girl answered, "My entire family was massacred." She heard the other girls' gasps.

"By Indians?" Samantha asked. Her face turned pale.

Daniel shook her head. "No, my ma was killed by the man we owed money to. Ma said we didn't have it but would by the time it was due. He beat her bad. She died a few days later. He came back the next week, and this time he brought men with him. They killed my pa and my brothers."

The two older girls couldn't believe what they were hearing. The girl before them had been so young when she had been left alone. They had been as well, but they had been blessed with friends who had taken care of them. Daniel, it seemed, had been left to her own raising. It was no wonder the girl was so untrusting.

As Maria studied the girl in a new light, she realized that she was shaking. *No wonder*, she thought silently. The girl's clothes, if you could call them that, were filthy and torn and couldn't be very warm. "Come on," she said. "Let's go someplace warmer."

Daniel took the lead and led them into the back room of the saloon. There, they talked for hours. Or at least, Samantha and Maria did. Daniel sat there, listening quietly, only talking when they spoke directly to her.

Finally, it grew dark, and they were preparing to leave. As they were walking out, a drunk pushed up against Samantha and started flirting with her. Samantha tried to get away, but the drunken man was too strong for her.

He leaned up closer and slurred something about her being pretty and wanting to buy her a drink. Horrified, she snapped, "Let go of me!"

Suddenly he did.

Samantha looked over to see Daniel. She had reached out and shoved the drunken man, who, already off balance, stumbled backward. Angered, the man grabbed a whiskey bottle and brought it down on the girl's head, sending shattered pieces of glass everywhere.

Daniel went down. As she lay on the floor, the man shoved a boot into her side.

"Stop!" Samantha cried. "Stop it!"

Her cry attracted the attention of the bartender.

"What's wrong with you?" he demanded. "Beating up on a child!" Then he roughly grabbed the man and hauled him outside.

As the man was being taken care of, Daniel rose shakily. Then without a word, she grabbed the two shaken girls by an arm and led them out of the building.

"I don't think we should ever go back there," Samantha said, forgetting how she found her earlier visit humorous. "It is not a place for proper young ladies."

Maria nodded in agreement. "It's too dangerous. Besides, my pa would have tanned my hide for going in there."

Daniel just shrugged. This earned her a strange glance from the eldest girl.

Standing there on the walkway, they stood silently for a few moments. Finally, Samantha said, "It's getting late." Her remark triggered the others into action, and they each said good night.

The two older girls headed to the hotel, and just as they reached the door, Maria looked back and saw Daniel limp her way down the street and duck into an alley.

Turning back to the girl who had stopped ahead of her, Maria said, "Samantha, why don't you go on inside. There's something I need to do before I turn in."

The older girl looked at her curiously. But she nodded silently and went inside.

As soon as she was alone, Maria walked back to the alley. There she saw the girl working at the job she had been doing earlier. For a while, Maria watched her dig through the trash. Her heart broke as the girl finally came up with a blanket that was mostly rotten.

There was a ripping sound as Daniel tore a hole in the blanket and slipped it over her head. She turned and suddenly caught sight of Maria standing there. The older girl barely managed to dodge in time to avoid being hit.

A howl went up as Daniel's fist met a brick wall. But it didn't stop her. Instead, she turned and would have attacked again, except Maria's voice stopped her.

"Daniel! It's Maria."

A change came over Daniel, and she stood there staring at Maria. The dark eyes seemed to pierce into the older girl's mind and soul, searching for the reason of her being there.

Not knowing what to say, Maria simply said, "I want you to come and stay in the hotel with me."

She waited for Daniel's reaction, which was just a silent shake of her head. "Look, it's too cold for you to stay out here. And it's getting colder by the minute."

She herself couldn't keep from shaking, so she knew Daniel must have been freezing. Therefore, Maria wasn't surprised when the girl moved and sat down against the wall, out of the cold wind.

Again, Daniel shook her head. "Wasn't planning on staying out here," she said. "I stay in a shack about two miles out of town."

Maria frowned. "I know that place. I used to play there when I was little. Last time I was there, it was falling apart." Then shaking her head, she said, "Anyway, it's too cold for you to travel tonight."

To her frustration, Daniel shook her head for a third time. "It'd be too much trouble. Besides, they don't like my kinds of people in there."

Maria was confused. "Your kind of people?" she asked.

Daniel smiled sadly. Then she looked down at the ground. "People with no money."

Maria nodded understandingly. "Well, you can stay with me in my room. It wouldn't be any trouble."

Maria reached down and pulled Daniel to her feet. To her surprise, Daniel allowed Maria to lead her to the hotel and up to her room.

Once there, she gently began pulling the glass shards from the girl's long dark-brown hair. Then at her insistence, Daniel cleaned up and then sat down to let Maria comb her hair out.

The motion brought back fond memories. As Maria stroked the brush and gently worked out the tangles, Daniel was taken back to a time when she had been with her family.

Daniel's brothers were sixteen years older than her. Despite the age difference, the three were very close and spent a lot of time together. Oftentimes, when their mother was ill, the boys would help the four-year-old get ready for bed.

At night, one of them would sit with her on their lap as they gently brushed out the dark wavey hair. They took much longer than it should have as they spent the time talking and telling each other stories.

This was one of Daniel's favorite memories. And the gentle hands of her brothers came to mind now.

The girl was suddenly brought back to the present when Maria began speaking to her.

"Were you hurt?"

Thinking for a moment, Daniel replied, "No, were you?" She unconsciously rubbed her hand, and Maria knew she was thinking about the events that occurred in the alley.

"No, but I meant in the saloon," Maria clarified.

This time, Daniel merely shook her head, and Maria knew she was done speaking.

It took a while, quite a while, but finally, Maria removed all the tangles and burrs from Daniel's hair. Then the two girls fell asleep.

CHAPTER 5

The Discovery

The next morning, the two girls met Samantha in the newly reopened dining room for breakfast. When they entered, the oldest of the three couldn't believe how different Daniel looked now that she wasn't covered in dirt. Samantha also noticed she was wearing a coat that must have been Maria's.

Samantha realized that she still wouldn't have fit into the circles that she and Jenifer associated with, but in a much simpler way, she was very pretty. But she was also intimidating. It was clear that she liked to take care of herself.

"You'll have to let me repay you somehow," Daniel said, pulling Samantha from her thoughts.

"That isn't necessary," Maria said, despite Daniel's objections. "I told you that last night."

Somehow, they moved on to the subject of last night's conversation. Maria and Samantha talked about their families, but Daniel remained silent on the subject. Finally, Maria said, "I have a picture of my parents. Would you like to see them?"

She pulled a chain from around her neck, and at the end of it, the two girls saw a locket.

Samantha's expression changed from curious to surprise. "I have a locket just like that!" she exclaimed, pulling hers out. They were identical.

"How strange is that?" she questioned. Maria nodded while Daniel watched silently. "Well, let me show you my parents," Maria said.

She opened her locket, and Samantha gasped. Even Daniel leaned forward to look at the tiny photograph. Maria stared at the two girls, wondering why they had reacted this way.

"These are…your parents?" Samantha finally stammered, her face pale.

"Yes," Maria answered. "Why?" she added, a bit defensively.

"B-because they look like my parents!" The older girl finally replied. She opened her own locket, and sure enough, the same tiny faces looked up at them.

"They're the same!" Maria gasped.

"But why?" Samantha questioned. "Why would we have identical lockets? With pictures of the same people?"

As they pondered this, Daniel silently slipped something from her pocket and pushed it toward the center of the table. It fell open, and the other two just stared at it. Just like the other girls, she had produced a locket with a picture of the couple staring up at them with loving smiles.

"My family told me I was adopted," Daniel said. "I never knew the man and woman from the pictures. But my parents said I had this when they adopted me. They assumed the people were my original parents."

The two girls stared at her. The way she said it was so detached it sounded like she was speaking of something that had happened to someone else. Yet the other two nodded. Their parents had told them the same thing.

Just then, Maria bolted to her feet. "Let's go," she said suddenly.

"Where?" Samantha asked. She too rose.

"To the courthouse. I want to see if there is any clue as to why we all have the same lockets with the same picture," Maria replied.

"You don't think…" Samantha began. But her voice trailed off before she could finish. *It's not possible*, she thought silently.

"We have to find out," Maria stated. She was so anxious to find answers to the questions that were now swirling in her mind that she forgot to look back and see if the other two were following. Apparently, they were since they appeared by her side when she reached the doors of the courthouse.

The girls went inside and spoke to the woman working there. Samantha explained their purpose there, and the woman smiled at them sadly. "I'm sorry, but doctors didn't keep records back then." She thought for a moment, then said, "You might ask at the orphanage. While doctors didn't keep records, the woman at the orphanage did. Perhaps she could help you."

After thanking the woman, they left the courthouse. When they reached the orphanage, which lay on the outskirts of town, they went inside and found the lady who was in charge.

She was an elderly woman in her late fifties. When she saw the three girls standing there, she smiled. But her eyes widened when she saw the lockets each wore around their necks. "Oh my," she whispered.

"Do you know us?" Daniel asked, instantly seeing the woman's reaction at their appearance.

"Why don't you come into the kitchen?" the woman said nervously. "We can talk over something hot to drink."

Soon, they were all sitting around an old wooden table in the kitchen.

"Do you know us?" Daniel asked again.

Taking a drink of her coffee, the woman nodded. "Yes, or at least, I know your lockets. Thirteen years ago, three little girls were brought in. Each had a matching locket.

"The eldest child was about two years old. The middle child was about one, and the youngest was barely a month. I was new here and had only been in operation for about two months, so I wasn't sure where the girls had come from. Someone had just left them on my step."

She paused and waited for their reactions. When none came, she continued, "It was a few months later when a man and woman came to adopt a baby girl. They were extremely interested in the eldest of the three girls. I said they had to take all of you, but they said they couldn't care for three, just one. They left without adopting any of you."

The woman looked up from her cup sadly. "It was always that way. Nobody was able to care for three little girls. Finally, you were all assigned to different homes. I felt terrible about splitting up a family, but I convinced myself that it was for the best."

The girls stared at her silently. "But…I've lived here all my life!" Maria managed. "How could you not tell me?"

"I couldn't bear to!" the woman exclaimed. "How could I tell you that I tore your family apart? Besides, you seemed so happy with your new parents."

The three girls were too stunned to speak. Finally, the woman looked up, with tears in her eyes. "Please believe me. I never would have done it if I thought I would have been able to find a home for all of you! People were still finding their way after the war, and it just wasn't going to happen. I just wanted to give you the best life possible!"

"What was our name?" Samantha asked. The others waited curiously for the answer.

"Your first names remained the same. But your last name was Michaels," the woman said with a sob.

Finally, the three girls were out of things to say, so they found an excuse to leave. When they were standing outside, it was Maria who broke the silence. "I guess this means we're sisters," she said seriously.

"I guess it does," Samantha agreed, excitement in her voice. "How old are you?" she asked.

"I'm fourteen," Maria replied. "What about you?"

"I am fifteen," Samantha answered. "Which would line up with the time frame the woman inside shared."

Turning to Daniel, she questioned, "How old are you?"

Daniel shrugged. "Thirteen," she said.

Maria shook her head. "I almost can't believe it… I mean…sisters! And our meeting after all this time!"

Samantha nodded. "It truly is amazing!" she exclaimed.

Suddenly Maria had a thought. "You both should come live with me on my ranch! That is, if you want to."

Samantha smiled. "That would be lovely! I would hate for us to part now that we've only found one another."

The two girls turned to see what Daniel had to say, but she was already halfway down the street. "Daniel! Wait up!" Maria called.

The girl did not look back. However, she did stop and lean against the hitching rail. The two older girls ran up to her.

"Daniel, why'd you take off so suddenly?" Maria asked.

Daniel shook her head. "No reason. I've just got things I need to get back to."

"Daniel! Maria has invited us to come live with her on her ranch!" Samantha exclaimed.

A worried expression came into the girl's dark, untrusting eyes.

"What's wrong?" Maria asked.

Daniel shrugged. "Just wondering why. Why would you open your home to a complete stranger?"

"You're not a complete stranger!" Maria exclaimed. "Daniel! You're my sister! And so is Samantha! That's why I want you both to live with me."

"It would be nice to have a family again," Daniel said slowly. "*Nice, but impossible*," she added silently. Aloud she continued, "But it would be too much trouble. We each have our own lives. To intrude on yours wouldn't be right."

This time, Maria didn't worry about how Daniel would react. She merely reached out and embraced the child. "Daniel, listen to me. We are sisters now. And not having you in my life would cause more pain, heartache, and trouble than anything else in the world."

Her words seemed to pierce the shield that the youngest girl had built around herself. "A-are you sure you want both of us to live with you?" she asked uncertainly.

"Yes!" Maria exclaimed. "I want you both to come home and live with me on my ranch, our ranch!"

Again, her words seemed to convince the child since she cautiously nodded and accepted Maria's offer of a home. "We'll stay in the hotel tonight," Maria decided, "and head home in the morning."

Home—even to her own ears the word sounded different, better somehow. She couldn't imagine what it must have meant to the others.

Still excited from their discovery, they walked over to Mr. Brown's store. "Mr. Brown!" Maria called.

Hearing the urgency in her voice, the storekeeper appeared instantly. "Maria, what's wrong?" he asked.

"Nothing's wrong!" Maria said, practically jumping up and down. "I have a family again!"

Shock registered on the man's elderly face. "What do you mean?" he asked.

Maria motioned toward the two girls. "We're sisters!" she exclaimed.

Mr. Brown's shock turned to joy. "Congratulations!" he exclaimed, sweeping the girl into a hug. "You must all sit down and tell me everything."

So the three girls followed him into the back room, and they sat down and told him everything. At least, Samantha and Maria did. Daniel just sat back, listening quietly.

"I'm so happy for all of you," he said at last once they had finished.

Soon it had grown late; and the three girls headed to the hotel, went to their rooms, and fell asleep.

When Maria awoke the next morning, she quickly looked for Daniel. But the youngest sister was not there. Nor was there any evidence she had stayed there during the night.

Quickly Maria went down to knock on Samantha's door. She quickly answered and saw Maria's worried expression.

"What's wrong?" she asked.

"Daniel's gone. She was in our room when I fell asleep last night. But she wasn't there when I awoke. And it looks like she didn't stay there last night either."

Samantha stepped into the hall. "Surely she didn't just leave."

Maria shrugged. "I can't imagine why she would."

But silently both girls were wondering.

The two girls left the hotel. Looking up and down the street, they spotted someone about Daniel's height coming out of the saloon. Hurrying up the boardwalk, they reached the girl, who stood leaning against a pole.

They noticed a bag at her feet, but they ignored it.

"Daniel, where have you been?" Maria questioned.

Without looking at her sisters, Daniel said, "I had to go home and get my belongings. I also had to tell Jake that I might have to work a different schedule. Then he needed someone to fill in for a couple hours. You weren't awake so…" She shrugged.

It was then that the two girls noticed how Daniel was dressed. She was wearing a purple dress that hung only to her knees. The bodice's neckline was low, though still much higher than that of the older women.

Samantha's gaze turned to the structure behind them. "Y-you work in the saloon?" She looked horrified.

Daniel nodded. "You should know that. I rescued you twice."

Samantha gasped. "Twice. Wait…that was you?"

Daniel nodded. "You attract more trouble than I do." She gave the first smile the two had seen from her.

"Daniel, you cannot keep working there! You're only thirteen!" Samantha exclaimed. "Besides, proper young ladies shouldn't work in places such as…such as…" She motioned behind her. "Such as that!"

Daniel's smile faded. "Good thing I'm not a proper lady. Besides, Jake was the only person who would hire me."

Samantha stepped back from Daniel and put a hand on her hips. "Daniel Michaels, you march right back in there and tell Mr. Jake that you won't be working for him anymore."

Daniel's expression darkened. "I won't do it, Samantha. And despite what you think, there is nothing going on beyond those doors than what normally goes on in a hotel bar." She picked up her bag and said, "I knew this was a mistake…" She turned her back and more quietly said, "I should have known better than to hope for…" She shook herself and started to head back inside. But she stopped when Maria placed a hand on her arm.

"Daniel, wait," she pleaded.

Daniel froze.

"Daniel," Maria began, "why did you start working in a saloon? Was it just for the money?"

The youngest girl refused to look at Samantha, focusing all her attention on Maria. "I already told you. Jake was the only person in town that would hire me. It takes money to live, and I don't have any."

Maria nodded. "Do you like working there?" she asked.

Daniel shook her head. "Does any girl? No, I do not like working there, but it's the only choice I have."

Maria suddenly smiled. "Then you don't have to worry about coming back here. If you want, you can work on the ranch. I draw a wage, just like the hired hands do. You could too."

Daniel seemed to think about it for a moment. Then her smile returned. "That would be nice. I hate this dress," she said.

Maria laughed.

Daniel turned to go back inside, but Samantha placed a hand on her shoulder.

"Daniel," she said softly.

Daniel stopped again, but she didn't look at her eldest sister. Nor did she speak.

"Daniel, I'm sorry. I didn't mean to snap. I was taught that girls who worked in saloons were…" She struggled to find the right word.

Daniel nodded. "I know what people say. I've heard it often enough. But we're not like them. All we do is sell drinks. And I sing, and others dance. We girls don't even drink. Most of the girls I work with would rather be somewhere else. But there just aren't very many choices. They aren't always lucky enough to find a family." She frowned for a moment, and then quietly she whispered, "But on that front, maybe they're the lucky ones. They can't lose what they've never had."

With that, she entered the saloon. While she was gone, Samantha sighed. "I guess I handled that badly."

Maria couldn't argue.

When Daniel returned, she was dressed in her normal street clothes. For a moment, all three girls stood there.

Then Maria asked, "Are you two ready to head home?"

Samantha and Daniel both smiled. "Homeward!" they both said.

CHAPTER 6
Christmas

T he next day, Maria awoke and went downstairs. Moving to the kitchen, she began fixing breakfast. As she worked, she thought about the events of yesterday.

She still couldn't believe it. She had sisters—sisters who had come to live with her!

After Daniel had officially quit working in the Desert Flower Saloon, the youngest and eldest girls had made up. Then Maria had brought the girls out to the Full Circle Ranch.

Upon their arrival, the first thing she did was take them into the house and allow them their choice of rooms. She had not been surprised by their choices.

Samantha had picked the spacious room that let in the most natural light. Daniel, on the other hand, had chosen a small room, with one window and a clear view of the road. It was also the one closest to the back stairway.

Once they had settled in, they spent the rest of the day riding across the ranch. Maria showed them the herds they owned. She talked about the land, and she showed them the fields that would be used for crops.

Throughout the tour, Maria explained what the work would be like. She said the two girls would start out with easier assignments. That way they could learn the ropes.

Daniel, having lived on a ranch with her family, caught on quickly, but it took a while for Samantha. They were watering the animals, and the eldest girl was worn out. She smiled and said, "I'm used to having pipes deliver the water."

That night, the girls had stayed up late into the night talking. It was near midnight when they had finally turned in.

Maria was suddenly pulled from her thoughts as Samantha entered the kitchen. "Something smells good."

"Good morning, Samantha," Maria greeted her sister.

"Good morning, Maria," Samantha returned. "Have you seen Daniel this morning?"

Maria shook her head. "No, I haven't. I'm sure she's around here somewhere."

Samantha shrugged. "Maybe she's still asleep."

Maria laughed. "Are you kidding? Don't you remember yesterday? She was gone before we even stirred. I doubt that girl has the problem of sleeping in."

Suddenly the front door opened, and the peacefulness of the morning was broken. "Let go of me!" Daniel's voice carried into the kitchen.

Glancing at each other, the two girls went to see what was happening. Reaching the entryway, they saw a young man holding Daniel by the hood of her worn jacket.

"Caleb, what in the world is going on?" Maria asked. As she waited for an answer, she took in the chaotic scene.

The teenager glanced up at Maria. "Sorry to barge in, Maria," he apologized. "I found this girl in the barn. Looks like she was trying to steal one of the horses. I couldn't find Mr. Thompson, so I thought I'd ask you where he was."

"I wasn't stealing the horses!" Daniel snapped. "*Now. Let. Me. Go.*" She delivered a sharp kick to Caleb's knee.

Crying out, he released Daniel and went down.

"Caleb, leave her alone," Maria said.

The boy groaned as he stood.

"Go out and gather the men. I have an announcement to make."

The boy limped out of the house, and Maria turned to Daniel. "Are you alright?" she asked.

Daniel nodded. "Yeah, I'm just glad I never had to fight against that boy. I would have gone hungry that night."

Samantha and Maria stared at her.

"You mean you fought for money?" Samantha exclaimed with a gasp.

Daniel smiled. "Maybe I'll explain it to you sometime," she said. *But I doubt it*, she thought, hoping that day never came.

A couple of minutes later, everyone was standing in the yard. Maria glanced around at the crowd and said, "Gentlemen, I would like to introduce you to my sisters." She smiled at the surprised expressions on the men's faces. "This is Samantha, my elder sister." She placed a hand on Samantha's shoulder. "And this is Daniel, my younger sister. They will be living and working on this ranch from now on. Also, they will be made partners of ownership."

Once she had introduced the two girls, Maria began introducing the men. She started with the foreman. "This is Mr. Thompson. He is my foreman and my legal guardian."

She was about to move on, but the foreman said, "Maria, I think you and I had better have a talk about this."

Neither missed the worried glances that passed between Samantha and Daniel.

Maria nodded. "We can talk over breakfast as soon as we are done here."

The next person in line was Thomas. As she introduced him, Maria explained that the new fields had been his idea. He blushed at her praise.

Then came Caleb. He and the three girls shared a smile and a laugh as they shook hands. Soon, everyone had been introduced.

As everyone went their separate ways, Maria led her sisters back to the house, followed by Mr. Thompson. As they sat down for breakfast, Maria, as always, said grace.

Finally, Mr. Thompson said, "Maria, what is this about these girls being your sisters? Your parents never had any other children."

Maria nodded. "As you know, Mr. Thompson, I was adopted by the people who raised me. I met these girls two days ago and discovered that we were indeed sisters."

By the time breakfast was over, Maria had explained everything—from the discovery of the lockets, to the inquiry at the courthouse, to the interrogation and confession of the lady who ran the orphanage.

Mr. Thompson whistled. "I'll say Maria, you had quite a full two days. And for being so young, you were very wise in how you went about this."

Maria smiled. "Thank you, Mr. Thompson."

The foreman nodded. "From what you've told me, I believe you are right. You three are sisters. However, I am going to do a bit of checking on my own."

Samantha spoke up before Maria could, "I thought you might, Mr. Thompson, especially when Maria mentioned you were her legal guardian."

A week later, Maria came into the house. Samantha stood in the kitchen, working on the noon meal, and she glanced up.

"You seem lost in thought," the older girl remarked.

Maria looked up and smiled. "I was just talking with the hands," she began, "and we got onto the subject of Christmas."

Samantha looked startled. "Is it that time already?" she asked.

Maria nodded.

"Wow! It was only November when I arrived in town."

Maria sat down in one of the chairs at the table. "What did you do for Christmas back in Boston?" she asked.

Samantha smiled. "My friend Jenifer and I went to parties. We were always the belles of the ball, so to speak. Everyone wanted to dance with us."

"I'm afraid we don't have parties that fancy here," Maria said. "But we do have a Christmas Eve service at church."

Suddenly her smile brightened.

"And that doesn't mean we can't have a party here."

Samantha frowned, slightly confused. "What?" she asked.

"A party is just a bunch of people getting together for a good time," Maria said. "We can do that here. It can be the three of us and the men!"

Now Samantha smiled. "It would be nice!" she said.

"What would be nice?" a new voice asked.

The two girls turned to see Daniel, who had just come in.

"A Christmas party!" Samantha said, clearly excited. "Here, at the ranch."

"Who will be here?" Daniel asked.

"Just us and the men," Maria assured her, realizing her sister didn't like crowds.

"Daniel, isn't it going to be grand?" Samantha asked. It was obvious to all that she was thrilled with the idea of a party.

Daniel shrugged. "I guess," she said. "I've never been to a party." As she leaned against the kitchen doorframe, she smiled at the shock on Samantha's face. "What?" Daniel asked, already knowing the answer.

"You…you've never been to a party?" Samantha gasped. She couldn't believe it.

Daniel shook her head. "I don't much like crowds," she answered.

Samantha shook her head. "I cannot believe it! Oh, Daniel, the parties in Boston were simply amazing, especially the Christmas balls! All the ladies would wear their best dresses, and the young men would be in their suites." Samantha smiled as she remembered the grand times she and Jenifer had spent at parties. "The finest musicians in Boston would play, and we would spend the night dancing."

Daniel smiled sarcastically. To her, it sounded like a waste of time, but she didn't say so. Instead, she said, "I guess it would be worth it, to get a free meal."

Maria laughed, and Samantha smiled, shaking her head.

Then the eldest girl asked, "What were your Christmases like?"

Daniel's smile turned from laughter to one of sad remembrance. "My family and I would spend the holiday together. Sitting in front of the fire, Pa would read the Christmas story. Then if the year had been good, we sometimes swapped gifts. But that didn't happen too often."

For a while, all were silent, then Maria spoke up, "How does this sound? Tomorrow is the nineteenth. Why don't we take Thomas and Caleb and go fetch a tree?"

Samantha nodded, saying, "That sounds wonderful, Maria."

Glancing over at Daniel, they noticed her dark eyes were sparkling with excitement.

Early the next morning, the girls and their escorts left the ranch. They spent the day looking for the perfect tree. Finally, they decided on a tall full pine.

Glancing at the tree, Thomas said, "Good choice, girls." Then he walked over to it with the axe. "Stand back. When this goes, it will go fast. We don't want any of you to get squished."

Everyone laughed as he chopped away at the tree trunk. About five minutes later, the tree fell with a crash. Thomas and Caleb grabbed hold of the trunk and, with the girls following, pulled it over to the sled.

Once they arrived back at the ranch, the boys carried the tree into the house.

"Move it to the right," Maria instructed.

"No, move it back," Samantha said.

"Move it southwest," Daniel stated.

Everyone looked up at her.

She glanced past them and nodded. "Yep, move it about half a foot to the southwest."

The boys did as she requested. Joining the girls, they looked at their handiwork. "It's perfect," Caleb said, stretching.

"Not quite," Maria said, smiling at their dismayed expressions. "If you two boys would be so kind, there are several boxes of Christmas decorations in the attic."

With playful moans, the boys left to fetch down the boxes. It didn't take long, and soon they left the girls to the decoration.

By the time they were finished that night, they were exhausted. "We'd better get some rest," Samantha said. "Tomorrow we'll have to go into town."

The younger girls looked at her. "I don't know about you," she said, "but I have some Christmas shopping to do."

Maria nodded. "Fine, we'll leave right after breakfast." Turning to Daniel, she said, "Is that alright with you?"

Daniel nodded. "I'll be ready," she promised.

And with that, the three girls headed upstairs and went to bed.

Early the next morning, the sisters rode to town. Daniel was the first to finish with her shopping. As she waited for her sisters, she spoke with Mr. Brown.

"And how is family life treating you, Daniel?" the storekeeper asked.

Daniel's smile answered for her. Yet she replied, "Really well, Mr. Brown."

Mr. Brown smiled back at her. "I'm glad to hear it. I was afraid you'd be alone this Christmas. In fact, I was planning on inviting you to spend the holidays with me."

Daniel smiled. "Thank you for the offer, Mr. Brown. It was nice of you to think of me."

Just then the sheriff entered the store.

"Hello, Sheriff," Daniel greeted him.

The sheriff smiled. "Why, Daniel, I hardly recognized you. You look a might different than when you spent the night in my jail, healthier too."

At that moment, Maria walked up. "You were arrested?" she asked. "When?"

Daniel smiled sheepishly. "Not too long after I hit town." Then she laughed. "You and Samantha aren't very observant."

At Maria's confused expression, Daniel said, "You looked right at me that day you came to visit the sheriff in the jail. You talked about the reverend and how he should keep his preaching in the church—"

Maria cut her off. "That was you?" she asked unbelievingly.

Daniel nodded. "Yep, that was me."

The two men couldn't contain their laughter. Maria and Daniel couldn't either. However, by the time Samantha finally finished, they had gotten it under control.

The girls paid for their items and then headed back to the ranch.

Soon it was Christmas Eve. At six o'clock, they told the ranch hands to come in. Together they supped on the goose Mr. Thompson had surprised them with.

When the meal was over, everyone gathered in the living room. Sitting before the fire, the three girls passed out the gifts they had bought the men.

As they received their gifts, each man sputtered a surprised and heartfelt thanks. Then the men also offered the girls the items they had purchased. Each was presented with a box of pretty handkerchiefs.

After the gifts had been exchanged, Maria went to the corner of the room and produced a guitar. Walking over to the foreman, she placed the instrument in his hands. "Play something we can dance to," she asked kindly.

Reaching out, Mr. Thompson took the guitar. He strummed it to make sure it was in tune. Then he began to play.

Because of the small size of the room, only a few people could dance at one time. Maria paired with Thomas, and Samantha danced with one of the other hands. When the song had finished, they thanked their partners.

Leaving the makeshift dance floor, the sisters smiled at one another. They walked over to Daniel, who had been watching the graceful movements of her sisters.

"Come on, Daniel," Samantha said, pulling the younger girl to her feet. "It's Christmas and the last song of the night. Give it a shot."

Daniel protested. "I've never danced at a party before," she said.

Maria smiled and said, "Well, there's a first time for everything." She gave her sister a shove, causing her to stumble into Caleb.

The boy smiled down at Daniel. Grinning, he said, "Might I have this dance?"

Daniel smiled up at him. "I guess. You may as well."

Samantha lifted one of her new handkerchiefs, given to her by the men, trying to hide her laughter. Maria glanced at the floor in an effort to do the same.

But then she heard Samantha quietly gasp "oh my." Looking back up, she saw what had surprised her older sister.

In the center of the room, Daniel gracefully danced with her partner. Her movement was fluid and natural, as was Caleb's.

Finally, the song ended, and Caleb escorted Daniel to her sisters.

Seeing their shocked expressions, Daniel said, "My ma taught my brothers to dance. And she taught me as soon as I could walk." Turning to Caleb, she said, "Before you go, I have one more gift for you."

Caleb smiled. "And I you."

They each pulled a small item from their pockets and stood there awkwardly.

"How about we open them at the same time?" Caleb suggested.

They counted to three and opened the boxes. Then they looked at each other, grinning. Each had given the other a wooden hand-carved barn pendant on a chain.

"In remembrance of our first meeting," Daniel said.

"When you tried to steal the horses," Caleb added with a smile.

"I wasn't stealing the horses. If I had been, you'd never have known I was there."

Each of the hands said good night, and the girls returned their partings with Christmas well-wishes. Then once more, they settled by the tree.

"Now for our gifts to one another," Samantha said. She handed one of the packages she had bought to each of her sisters. She received one gift from each girl in return.

Together they opened their gifts. Samantha had given Maria a tiny horse charm. To Daniel, she gave a mystery book.

Maria gave Samantha the sequel to the book the older girl had been reading when they first met. She gave Daniel a new coat.

Daniel gave both of her sisters the same item. Both received new chains for their lockets.

That night, as they camped out beside the tree, Daniel said, "You know what?"

"What?" Samantha and Maria asked at the same time.

"I already had my Christmas gift," Daniel said softly.

Samantha rolled over and propped herself up on her arm. "What was that?" she asked.

Daniel continued to stare up at the tree. She was quiet for so long the older girls thought she wasn't going to answer. Finally, she answered, "I got a family again."

From either side of her, the two older girls exchanged smiles. Each had been thinking the same thing.

"Us too, Daniel," Maria said. "Us too."

CHAPTER 7
Boston

The months passed, and soon, spring had arrived. Samantha stood in the kitchen, reading a letter she had received from Boston.

She was reading so intently that she didn't notice Daniel standing across from her. Finishing her letter, she glanced up and jumped.

"Oh, Daniel! You startled me! I didn't see you standing there."

Daniel smiled and accepted the cup that Samantha offered her. Silently she sipped the drink and contemplated how each sister's preference reflected their different personalities. Samantha always made tea, a more delicate drink from the east. Maria, on the other hand, always made coffee, a favorite of the west. Then she realized that her sister was speaking to her.

"The letter was from Jenifer, the friend I first arrived with," Samantha explained. "She wants me to come and visit her now that the cold weather has passed."

Daniel nodded. "Must be nice to have friends to visit. How long will you be gone?" She didn't notice Samantha's smile.

"Well," the older girl began, "it is a three-day journey there by train. Then I thought we would stay for a week while I show you around Boston. Then it would be three days back. I figure we'd be gone about two weeks."

Just then Maria entered the kitchen. "Good morning," she greeted her sisters.

Each returned the greeting, and Maria spotted the letter. "News from Boston?" she asked.

Samantha nodded. She repeated what she had just told Daniel.

Maria said, "I've never been to Boston. It sounds exciting."

"Oh, it is!" Samantha exclaimed. "You'll just love it!" In her excitement, she didn't notice her youngest sister thinking.

"Two weeks," Daniel said to herself. "I can get the horses ready for the army. Don't really know much about the dealings, but Mr. Thompson could probably take care of that… been meaning to patch the shack's roof…" Suddenly she got the feeling that both sisters were staring at her. Glancing up, she met their gazes. "What?" she asked.

Samantha smiled. "Daniel! It's going to be hard fixing the roof all the way from Boston!"

The youngest girl shrugged. "Wasn't planning on going."

Samantha's smile disappeared. "Not planning on going?" she asked. "Why not?"

Daniel glanced up at her. "It would take too long to get there by horse. And I can't afford the train."

Maria placed a hand on her shoulder. "Don't worry about it, Daniel. We sold enough horses last year to cover a trip to Boston. Actually, Mr. Thompson was planning on taking a business trip there."

Since Daniel had brought up the cost, Samantha had been thinking. "I have money in a Boston bank. It will more than cover the train fair. I'll purchase the tickets."

Daniel studied her two sisters for a long moment. It seemed as if she were trying to think of some reason why she couldn't join them. Finally, she smiled softly. "I've never been to a big city before."

Samantha hugged Daniel. "I'm sure you'll enjoy it," she said excitedly. She wrote a letter to her friend, announcing that they would be coming. She also noted the date of her arrival.

The morning they were going to leave, Samantha packed her bags. Her sisters were shocked when she loaded two suitcases in the wagon. She was also carrying a handbag.

Maria only took one suitcase and a saddlebag. Daniel only carried one bag. As she tossed it into the bed of the wagon, Maria noticed it was the same one she had appeared with that morning outside the saloon.

"I like to travel light," Daniel explained when Samantha remarked about the small bag.

Finally, they were ready, and an hour later, they arrived at the train station. There they purchased their tickets and allowed their luggage to be loaded.

When the train pulled away from the station, the girls settled in for the long ride. They had only been traveling for about ten minutes when Maria glanced over at her sisters.

Samantha was reading a book to her left. Daniel, on the other hand, was stretched out on the floor of the train between the rows of seats, asleep. Maria laughed, drawing Samantha's attention. She pointed to her sister, and the eldest girl laughed as well.

The three-day journey was a long and rather-boring event. On the second day of their travel, Daniel returned from once again prowling the train cars. She sat down beside Samantha and closed her eyes.

"Are you planning on sleeping the entire journey away?" the elder girl asked teasingly.

Daniel didn't move except to reply. "Not much else to do. I already covered the train twice. I checked out the passengers again as well. No one on board is a danger to us."

Samantha hesitated, surprised by her sister's words. Then she reached into her handbag and retrieved a book. "Here. This is one of my favorites. It might help to pass the time."

Again, she hesitated. Then she asked, "You can read, can't you?" As she voiced the question, her mind flashed back to the book she had given her sister for Christmas.

Daniel laughed. "Yes, I read. My brothers taught me." She paused, and her smile faded. "After they were gone, it became an escape."

She didn't explain the statement, and Samantha didn't ask her too. Instead, both turned to the books in their hands.

The train chugged its way across the country. Finally, after another full day of travel, it made its final stop in front of the Boston Train Station.

As they stood on the platform, Samantha looked around. Suddenly she exclaimed, "There's Jenifer and Uncle Paul!" Then she took off running.

As they followed, Maria and Daniel shared a laughing smile at Samantha's excitement.

The two girls embraced.

"Samantha!" Jenifer exclaimed.

Embracing her friend, the Boston girl said, "You are certainly looking well."

Samantha returned the embrace and examined her friend. "And you as well! Why, I believe you've gotten taller."

Suddenly Samantha remembered the two girls who were hanging back behind her. "Jenifer, Uncle Paul," she said, moving to stand between the girls, "these are my sisters. This is Maria, second eldest, and Daniel, the youngest."

Jenifer nodded politely at each girl. "It's a pleasure to meet you," she said. Looking at Maria, she asked, "You're the rancher. Is that correct?"

Maria nodded. "Yes, I own a ranch. We raise horses to sell them to the army."

Jenifer nodded. "What type of horses?" she inquired.

"Morgens mostly," Maria explained. She briefly explained the workings of the ranch.

Mr. Stone stepped forward and shook hands with Mr. Thompson. "And it is a pleasure to meet you as well, Mr. Thompson. Samantha has mentioned you in her letters to us."

The foreman shook hands with Mr. Stone. "And she has told us a great deal about you, Mr. Stone, most importantly, how you took her in after her parents died."

Mr. Stone glanced over at the girls. "From what Samantha tell us in her letters, it was no more than what you did for Miss Michaels."

Glancing over at Daniel, Jenifer said, "It's too bad that you didn't have anyone to care for you." She smiled while she spoke, but Daniel caught the cruelty in her eyes.

Whatever she had expected the youngest girl to say, the reply Daniel gave was not it. She was quite surprised when the small girl said, "People cared." Then she turned away from Jenifer and stood by her sisters.

As they were stepping into the awaiting carriage, Jenifer thought, *I can't imagine what Samantha was thinking, acknowledging a girl like that as a relative. I guess I'll have to be the one to set her straight.*

The Stones' house was not far from the train station. The ride only took five minutes, and soon the girls were looking up at an impressive two-story stone structure.

"You never said you lived in a castle!" Maria exclaimed, laughing.

Jenifer smiled. "I guess it is bigger than what you are used to," she said.

As they entered the house, Jenifer walked beside Samantha. "As soon as I heard you were coming, I looked for things we could do together."

Samantha smiled at her friend. "Jenifer, I am planning on showing my sisters the city while we are here," she reminded gently.

"Why, there will be plenty of time for that," Jenifer assured her. "But tomorrow night, a play called *The Twelfth Night* is being shown. It was written by William Shakespeare in the early 1600s, I believe."

Samantha turned to her sisters. "Would you two be interested in seeing a play?" she asked.

Jenifer frowned. "Samantha, from what you've written, I'm not sure the girls would enjoy the play. It's rather long and sophisticated. Perhaps they would rather go with Mr. Thompson and attend to business pertaining to the ranch."

If Samantha noticed the insult, she made no mention of it. Before she could say anything however, Maria spoke up, "How much does it cost?"

They were surprised to hear Mr. Stone behind them. "Don't worry about the cost, girls. I told Jenifer that I'd pay for anything you girls enjoy while you are here."

"And that includes new gowns!" Jenifer said excitedly. "I'm sure you'll want something new, Samantha. The fashions changed quite a bit while you were gone."

The group had come to the parlor by this time, and Daniel noticed a woman sitting in a chair by the fireplace. "Hello," she said softly.

Everyone stopped talking and turned to see who she had spoken to. "Hello," the woman replied. "You must be Daniel."

"And you must be Mrs. Stone," Daniel replied with a smile.

"Yes, I am Mrs. Celia Stone. I must apologize for not meeting you at the station. I'm afraid I couldn't make it as I injured my foot last week and it's still painful to walk on."

Samantha stepped forward then. "I'm sorry to hear that, Aunt Celia."

The two embraced warmly.

"Since you've already met my youngest sister, allow me to introduce you to Maria," Samantha said, motioning to her sister.

Maria stepped forward. "It is nice to meet you Mrs. Stone." She shook hands with the woman.

They spoke for a few minutes, and then Celia looked at her daughter. "Jenifer, why don't you escort the girls to their rooms? I'm sure they would like to freshen up after the long ride."

Jenifer glanced up from where she sat talking with Samantha. "Yes, Mother," she answered.

Standing, she grasped Samantha's hand. "Come on! You're staying in your old room. I wouldn't let Mother and Father change it. I said you'd want it when you came back."

She took off, with Samantha following close behind. They could hear the girls laughing and talking as they ascended the stairs.

"I'm sorry about that," Mrs. Stone apologized. "My daughter has been so excited about your visit. She and Samantha were like sisters, and it has been hard for her since Samantha left."

She pulled a cord that hung on a nearby wall, and a dark-skinned girl soon appeared. "Ella, would you please take Miss Maria and Miss Daniel to their rooms? Once they have freshened up, you may escort them back here."

"Yes, ma'am," Ella replied. She turned to the two sisters. "Would you please follow me?"

They followed the young servant upstairs. They passed by several closed doors until they reached the end of the hall.

There, Ella let them into two rooms and indicated that they should pull the gold-colored cord on the wall when they were ready to head downstairs. When she was gone, the girls entered their rooms.

Down the hall from them, Samantha set about freshening up. She had already washed the travel dust away from her hands and face, and now she was donning a new gown.

"I remember that dress," Jenifer remarked. "You wore it to Sarah Mathews' birthday party."

Samantha laughed. "That was the time when her brother drank so much punch that he got sick. I felt bad for the little boy."

As she tugged the dress into place, Samantha heard her friend become quiet. When she turned around, she saw Jenifer looking at her. "What?" she asked.

"I missed you, Samantha. I'm glad you're home," Jenifer replied.

Something about Jenifer's words troubled Samantha. She wondered briefly what it could be, but then the feeling was forgotten when they headed back downstairs.

CHAPTER 8

The Play

The next morning, Samantha awoke early, despite having stayed up late reminiscing with Jenifer. Rising, she quickly dressed for the day and ventured downstairs. To her surprise, everyone was already awake and in the parlor.

As she entered, Jenifer rose. "Samantha, you're finally awake!" she exclaimed. "Now we can have breakfast and be off to the dress shop."

Samantha laughed as she recalled the plans that had been made at dinner last night. Since the play was to take place that evening, the girls had decided to purchase their gowns right after breakfast.

"Yes! I can hardly wait! It's been so long since I've had an occasion to wear such fancy outfits."

As the group rose to enter the dining room, Mr. Stone called his daughter to him. "Jenifer," he said, "before you and the girls leave, your mother and I have something to discuss with you in the library."

Jenifer nodded. "Alright, Father," she replied. Then she went to take her seat beside Samantha.

After they had finished their morning meal, Jenifer turned to Samantha. "Why don't you have the carriage brought around? I must speak with my parents for a few moments, and then I'll be out."

Samantha nodded and led her sisters outside. Jenifer watched them go and then turned and headed to the library.

"You said you wanted to speak with me, Father?" Jenifer asked as she entered.

Mr. Stone helped his wife into a chair and then turned to his daughter. "Yes" was all he said. For a moment, he studied his only child and then began pacing. "Jenifer, you've done very well in your studies at Windsor Finishing School. For that, your mother and I are very proud."

Jenifer smiled. "Thank you, Father," she said.

Mr. Stone continued, "Your teachers say that already you show the proper graces and etiquette that a young lady should show in society." He paused in his pacing and said, "However, both your mother and I have to disagree with their sentiments."

Jenifer was startled. This was not what she had expected her father to say. "F-Father?" she stammered.

Mrs. Stone spoke then, "Jenifer, a young lady is expected to know the proper manners and etiquette for every social situation. Having Samantha and her sisters in our home qualifies as a social situation, one in which you have greatly disappointed us."

Jenifer was so stunned she could hardly speak. When she found her voice, she could only question, "But…Mother, how could I have disappointed you?"

Mrs. Stone looked sadly at her daughter. "Jenifer, your father and I have heard some of the things you've said to Maria and Daniel. We've seen the way you treat them. These actions are not that of a young lady but rather a snobbish aristocrat. I would like to believe that was not the way you were raised."

Jenifer frowned. "But, Mother, I've only been trying to show Samantha the truth. These girls are not fit to be associated with! Samantha was a fool to even consider the possibility of being related to them."

"And what makes them so unfit?" Mr. Stone demanded of his daughter. "The fact that they were willing to do what it took for them to survive? The fact that they kept going even when everything was taken from them not once but twice?"

Mrs. Stone reached out to her daughter. "Jenifer, it is not how much money a person has that makes them rich. Those girls will be wealthier than you've ever dreamed of being because they found something worth holding on to—one another."

She paused to make sure Jenifer was listening. She appeared to be, but the girl's expression was less than understanding.

"And as for being in such a low class, perhaps you've forgotten the stories your father used to tell—how even as a boy he worked long hours in the factories, barely able to make a living. And yet we were able to rise above that social position until we were one of the most prominent families in Boston. Being socially fit means more than having money or power. It really means being kind and caring to those around you."

Mr. Stone laid a hand on his daughter's shoulder and said, "The girls are waiting. Now I expect you to be thinking about what we've said. Take care in how you treat them—*all* of them. Be the kind, loving young lady we've raised you to be."

With this dismissal, Jenifer turned and fled the room. Mr. Stone turned to his wife. "She's angry," he said.

Mrs. Stone nodded. "Yes," she agreed, "and she'll lose everything if she doesn't see the truth."

After leaving her parents, Jenifer went back up to her room. She stood there for a few minutes, trying to get her raging emotions under control. Finally, when she had calmed down, she washed her face and headed out to the front porch.

There she found the girls talking and laughing. It made a surge of anger course through her, but she hid it. "Are you ready?" she asked Samantha.

Samantha rose and nodded excitedly. "Yes, I'm not sure about my sisters, but I can't wait to try on the new gowns."

Maria nodded and then laughed when Daniel made a disgusted expression. "It won't be so bad," she told the girl.

The girls climbed into the carriage, and Jenifer tried to keep Samantha's attention. However, the girl often interrupted their conversation to point out things they passed to her sisters.

At last, the carriage stopped in front of La Belle Tréssor. "The Beautiful Treasure," Samantha interpreted.

"Yes," Jenifer said, stepping out of the carriage, "Madam Lilly Levasseur always carries the best gowns."

They were about to enter the shop when another establishment caught Samantha's eye. "You know what?" she exclaimed. "We should get a new picture for our lockets!"

Maria smiled brightly. "Yes! One of the three of us!"

Samantha was so excited; she grabbed her sisters' hands and pulled them into the shop.

Once inside, Samantha rang the little bell on the counter. A moment later, a man appeared, holding a camera.

"Yes? How many I help you young ladies this morning?" he asked.

Samantha spoke for the group, "My sisters and I were hoping to have a picture taken. We would like to put it inside our lockets."

She showed him her locket, and the man traced his mustache with his fingers. "I see," he said.

Daniel nudged Maria and said, "How long does it take to make the picture? And how much will it cost?"

She spoke quietly, but the man overheard her. "Two very good questions, young lady. As to your first inquiry, when photographs were first being produced, daguerreotypes required twenty minutes of exposure, and people had to remain perfectly still for several minutes at least." He smiled at Daniel's confused expression. "However," he added, "since then, improvements to the process have been made. And nowadays, photos only take twenty seconds of exposure, and the subjects only need to remain still for one minute."

Daniel nodded. "And the cost?" she inquired.

The man thought for a moment. "Fifty cents a photo."

Daniel glanced over at Samantha who nodded. "Alright," she said. "Show us what to do."

The man laughed and said, "Step this way, ladies."

The man had told the truth. Before they knew it, the girls' photograph had been taken, and the pictures were fitted to their lockets.

As he returned the lockets to the girls, they each thanked him politely. Daniel wanted to stay and ask more questions on how the pictures appeared on the camera slides, but her sisters led her over to the dress shop.

They entered the store and were welcomed immediately by a middle-aged woman. "Welcome to La Belle Tréssor," the woman said. "How may I assist you today?" She studied the four girls as she spoke.

"Madam Levasseur, we are in need of some formal gowns for an outing this evening," Jenifer explained.

"And might I ask what type of outing you young ladies will be attending?" Madam Levasseur asked.

"We will be attending a play this evening," Samantha explained. "*The Twelfth Night* by William Shakespeare."

"I see," Madam Levasseur said, nodding. She clapped her hands, and three women appeared. "Show these girls to the dressing rooms," she ordered.

Soon, the shop came alive with movement. The girls were brought gown after gown. Neither Maria nor Daniel could believe how many choices they were presented with.

An hour after the process, Daniel decided she had had enough. Much to Madam Levasseur's horror, she chose a tea gown of aesthetic style.

"But, mademoiselle, this gown is not appropriate to wear to such a formal outing. It was meant to be worn at home, visiting with only female companions."

Still, Daniel put her foot down and kept the brown-and-maroon gown. She was intrigued by the medieval bands of embroidery. Therefore, Madam Levasseur provided the thirteen-year-old with a loose-fitting corset.

Having made her choice, Daniel found a chair and promptly fell asleep. Maria finished soon after her younger sister. She had decided on a golden Victorian-style gown. Its simple style was comfortable yet elegant enough for evening wear. She handed the gown to Madam Levasseur and took a seat beside Daniel.

Two hours later, Samantha and Jenifer appeared. Maria poked Daniel, waking the younger girl. Then the sisters studied the two girls before them.

"What do you think?" Samantha inquired.

She wore a gown of gray-blue material, with a full bell-shaped skirt and sleeves that came off the shoulders.

"Looks mighty cold," Daniel said with a shrug. "But it suits you."

Maria nodded. "It's beautiful, Samantha," she encouraged her older sister.

Jenifer wore a dress of the same style. However, hers was a daring emerald green. The three sisters had to agree that she looked most becoming.

Madam Levasseur was pleased with their choices. "Most appropriate choices, girls!" she exclaimed. "The fabrics complement your complexions most adequately."

Samantha and Jenifer went back to change into their original dresses, and Madam Levasseur packed the gowns into garment bags.

When the girls returned, she said, "I will have these gowns delivered to your home, Mademoiselle Stone. They will be pressed and ready for this evening."

Jenifer thanked the woman and then led the girls out onto the street. "That took less time than I expected," Jenifer said once they were outside. "It's only twelve thirty. The play will not begin until eight o'clock."

Samantha smiled. "Then we have some time for sight-seeing." She took the lead and led the girls through the streets of Boston. Finally, they reached a large public garden.

"Oh wow!" Maria exclaimed. "This is beautiful."

"Yes," Samantha agreed, "some college students planted it in 1865 to honor the fallen soldiers and President Lincoln."

Jenifer nodded. "Each year a different school takes their turn planting and caring for the flowers. This year, it's the responsibility of Windsor Finishing School, where I attend."

After leaving the gardens, Samantha led them to a large gray-stone building. "This is the Baptist church were we always attended. I'm excited to visit it again on Sunday."

Next, they saw the library, and neither Maria nor Daniel could believe the number of books the building contained.

Samantha laughed at their awed expressions. "I spent a lot of time here, reading every book I could."

After leaving the library, they went to the cemetery where a war hero was buried. After explaining about the man, Samantha showed them where her adopted parents were buried.

Finally, she led them to a dock and explained that later in the week, they could take a riverboat ride.

At last, it was time to return to the Stones' house and prepare for the theater. Upon their arrival, the girls ate a quick snack and headed upstairs to bathe and dress for the evening. After each girl had finished dressing, Mrs. Stone sent Ella up to fix their hair.

The servant girl worked quickly and efficiently. Soon, she was escorting the four girls downstairs.

As they entered the parlor, Mrs. Stone looked up from her needlework. "Oh my!" she exclaimed. "You all look lovely."

They all thanked her, and then Jenifer said, "We must be going if we are to get a good seat."

Once again, they all loaded into the carriage and were on their way.

It was a fifteen-minute drive to the theater, and by the time they arrived, the girls had to hurry to their seats. As they headed for the auditorium, Samantha collided with someone.

"Oh!" Samantha exclaimed, losing her balance. She started to fall, but a hand wrapped around her arm and kept her upright. When she was once again steady on her feet, she looked up to see a boy around her age.

"I'm so sorry," she apologized.

The boy smiled down at her. "I'm not," he said. Then he laughed at her startled expression. The boy grinned. "If we had not run into each other, we never would have met."

"Officially, we still haven't," Samantha replied, laughing.

The boy smiled and said, "Allow me to remedy that situation." Then he bowed gallantly and said, "I'm James Clayton."

Samantha couldn't help but laugh. "Are you in the play, Mr. Clayton?" she asked.

Again, James smiled. "No, I came to watch."

"Alone?" Samantha asked, somewhat surprised.

James nodded. "Yes, a friend of mine was supposed to attend with me, but he became ill."

"I hope it's nothing serious," Samantha said sincerely.

"No, nothing too serious," James assured her. "Just an early spring cold."

Suddenly Samantha remembered to introduce herself. She was about to invite James to sit with them when Jenifer appeared at her arm. "Samantha, we must hurry if we are to get to our seats in time."

With that, Samantha was pulled into the auditorium. As she allowed herself to be guided along, Samantha cast an apologizing smile back at James, who bowed slightly in return. She laughed and then turned to follow Jenifer.

They made it just in time. And as they settled in, the curtain rose, and the play began. The music had just begun when someone came and took a seat beside Samantha. Glancing over, she was surprised at who it was.

James leaned over and said, "I believe this is the only Shakespearean play to both open and close with a music number."

Samantha smiled slightly and said, "That is interesting. I wonder why."

For the next three hours, the two enjoyed themselves. They laughed at the play and shared whispered thoughts throughout the entire production. When the final curtain dropped, they rose to leave.

Once outside the theater, Samantha turned to her knew friend. "I thought it was a wonderful play. Didn't you?" she asked.

James thought for a moment. Then he agreed, "It was enjoyable." He hesitated. "But might I be so bold as to say that the company made it more so."

Samantha felt herself blush. Hurriedly she said, "It's rather late. I'm afraid we must be headed home."

James looked over at her with a smile. "Then there isn't much time. I know we've only just met, but could I see you again?"

Samantha hesitated, them shook her head. "That would be nice, but I'm afraid I'm only going to be here for a week—

five more days actually. Then my sisters and I are returning home."

James nodded. "I see. Then it's been a pleasure to meet you."

He was about to leave, and impulsively Samantha said, "I am planning on showing my sisters the city before we leave. Perhaps you would like to join us."

James smiled brightly. "I would love to," he spoke.

"Good," Samantha said. "We are planning on going sightseeing tomorrow afternoon. If you come at one o'clock, we'll be ready."

James bowed again with a teasing smile. "Then I shall see you at one." After accepting the slip of paper with the address written on it, he handed her into the coach.

As the carriage made its way back to the Stones' house, Samantha found herself excited for their outing tomorrow. Her thoughts were suddenly interrupted by Jenifer.

"Samantha, who was that?" the Boston girl asked.

"Who was who?" Samantha asked distractedly.

"The young man you were speaking with," Jenifer clarified. "The one who sat next to you during the play."

"Oh, that was James Clayton," Samantha replied. She then explained how she had run into James and how she had invited him to join them as they toured the city.

Jenifer was shocked. "Samantha, how could you even consider such a thing? It isn't proper to be escorted by a young man unchaperoned. Why, you don't know anything about him!"

Samantha met her friend's gaze. "Which is why I invited him along! How can we know a person until we've spent some time with them?"

Jenifer sat back in her seat. She considered Samantha's words and then sighed. "It's just that I'm worried about you."

Samantha was shocked. "Worried about me; but why?"

Realizing this would be the best chance she had getting her friend to see just how dreadful a mistake she was making, Jenifer plunged ahead. "Because lately you haven't been showing good judgement. You go out West to have an adventure, then you come back with a rancher and a saloon girl whom you claim as relatives. That has already damaged your social position. Now you want to take up with a strange young man unchaperoned. Do you know what people will think, what they will say?"

Samantha's heart sank. She was silent for several moments and then said, "Jenifer, this isn't about me. This is about you. If you are too ashamed, too conceited to be seen with me and my sisters…" She paused. "I thought you would be happy for me. I finally found what I had lost."

"Samantha! You can't lose what you never had!" Jenifer exclaimed. "Those girls aren't your family. Maybe by blood, but there's more to family than that. *I'm* your family. Mother and Father raised you when your own parents died. *They* are your family, not some rift-raft from out West. All they can do is drag you down. You'll never get anywhere in society by publicly claiming them as relatives."

Samantha felt a tear slip from the corner of her eye. "Is this why you've been so rude to them? Why you've been so determined to put them down?"

Jenifer nodded silently.

"I'm disappointed in you, Jenifer. I thought you were a true friend," Samantha said.

"I…I am a true friend," Jenifer cried. "I was only watching out for your interest."

"No, you were watching out for your own," Samantha said. "You were so jealous of the love I have for my sisters that you forgot about the love I had for you. You and I were sisters Jenifer, but you've thrown that away. All you could see is what those girls could have taken from you. But you've taken more from yourself than they ever could."

Jenifer stared at the carriage floor. "Th-that's what Father said," she whispered. "But I wouldn't listen."

They had reached the Stones' house by this point. Now they were waiting to leave the carriage. Jenifer looked back at Samantha. "I…I'm sorry Samantha."

Samantha returned her gaze steadily. "So am I, Jenifer."

Those words sent Jenifer fleeing from the carriage. She ran up to the front steps of her home and slammed the door behind her before running up to her room and shutting that door with a bang as well.

Samantha left the carriage and entered the house more quietly than Jenifer had. Glancing up from the floor, she saw Mr. and Mrs. Stone in the parlor.

"Is something wrong, dear?" Mrs. Stone asked.

Samantha entered the parlor and said, "Yes, Aunt Celia, I'm afraid there is." She didn't want to explain everything, so she said, "Jenifer and I had a serious disagreement." She tried for a smile.

The Stones glanced at each other.

"It was about your sisters, wasn't it?" Mrs. Stone asked kindly.

Samantha nodded. "I'll have to talk to the girls about this. We may be moving to the hotel with Mr. Thompson tomorrow evening."

Mrs. Stone looked at the girl. "I hope you know you're always welcome here."

Samantha smiled. "I don't want to leave, but I believe it might be for the best."

Mrs. Stone cleared his throat. "I'm sorry you feel that way, Samantha, though I can't say we didn't see it coming."

Samantha shook her head. "I just wish I had." She looked up at her hosts and said, "I believe I'll turn in. Good night."

The couple bade her good night and watched her walk sadly up the stairs.

"I hate to think this way," Mrs. Stone said. "But I'm sorry they ever came back to Boston."

CHAPTER 9
A Tragic Ride

It only took Maria and Daniel twenty minutes to walk from the theater to the Stone Mansion. As they walked, they discussed the play. The jovial banter stopped however when Daniel said, "I'm going home tomorrow."

Maria stopped and stared at her sister. "But why? We've only been here one full day."

When Daniel fell silent, Maria turned her so they faced each other. "Daniel, what's wrong?" she asked.

Daniel sighed. "Four years may not seem like a long time, but when you're on your own, you learn a lot quickly. One thing I learned was how to read people."

"And?" Maria pressed.

"Jenifer doesn't like us, either one of us," Daniel finally said. "It's going to tear her and Samantha apart."

Maria nodded. "I see," she agreed. "But I think Jenifer's plan was to drive a wedge between Samantha and us, not herself."

Daniel shook her head sadly. "If one happens, so doesn't the other."

"Then we won't let it happen," Maria stated.

Daniel looked doubtful but nodded.

A few minutes later, they reached the mansion. Entering, they found it dark and deserted. Climbing the stairs, they headed for their rooms.

As they passed Samantha's door, they noticed a soft light underneath. "Let's get changed and then go talk to her," Maria suggested. She didn't want to give Daniel the chance to change her mind and leave on the morning train.

The younger girl shrugged and then disappeared into her room. Maria followed suit, and the two changed quickly. They met in the hall a few moments later and started for their sister's room.

Maria had just knocked when a quiet sound caught Daniel's attention. "You go ahead," she said softly. "I'll be there in a while."

Maria glanced down at her younger sister, but the girl's expression held no hints to explain her thoughts. Therefore, she simply stepped inside, calling, "Samantha, it's Maria."

Once she was gone, Daniel started down the hall. As she reached the door to Jenifer's room, she heard a quiet sob. Immediately she recognized it as the sound she had heard before.

Unlike Maria, Daniel didn't bother to knock. Finding the door unlocked, she pushed it open and entered the room. There, she found the Boston girl draped over her bed, sobbing.

Silently Daniel took a seat on the floor beside the bed and waited for the girl to realize she was there. She didn't have to wait long. As Daniel leaned against the bed, Jenifer looked up and blinked through the tears.

"W-what are you doing here?" she stammered.

Daniel shrugged. "I heard someone crying. I came to see what was wrong."

Startled, Jenifer looked up and said, "Everything is wrong." She crawled off the bed and sat beside Daniel. "They were right," she said, another sob escaping. "They were right, and now I've lost everything."

She glanced up at Daniel and saw that the younger girl was waiting for her to continue. "Do you remember how my parents wanted to talk after breakfast?"

Daniel nodded silently, and Jenifer continued, "They said I would lose what mattered most if…if I couldn't control my hate. But I wouldn't listen."

She paused, and when Daniel said nothing, Jenifer laughed sadly. "You don't talk very much."

Daniel only smiled.

"I never knew I could hate so much," Jenifer began. "But you and Maria threatened everything I knew. I was so jealous of how close you were to Samantha. I thought that if Samantha went back West with you, she'd forget about me. So I…I tried to show her how you were…were socially unfit to be associated with. Then maybe she'd stay here and take her place in society with me. We…we could be sisters again."

A sob cut her off. When she recovered slightly, she continued, "My parents saw this coming, but I was blinded by hate. I've pushed my best friend away because I was so foolish." She hid her face in her hands and wept.

She was startled by a voice. In her sorrow, she had almost forgotten Daniel was in the room. She jumped when the younger girl spoke.

"Have you told this to Samantha?"

Jenifer shook her head. "We fought during the carriage ride home. We haven't seen each other since then." The girl sighed. "She'll probably never speak to me again." Then she peeked up at Daniel. "I can't believe your speaking to me, after the way I've treated you."

Daniel frowned and said, "I know what it's like to lose people you care about. I also know that if your plan had worked, we would have all lost Samantha. That's why

I'm here. So we can settle our differences. Then we'll talk to Samantha."

Jenifer let her head fall onto her arms, which were resting on her knees. "But what if she doesn't want to talk?"

Daniel smiled. "If Maria and I wouldn't let you ruin our relationship with Samantha, what makes you think we'll let her ruin it herself? And with you beside us, she doesn't stand a chance."

For the first time that evening, Jenifer smiled. "Thank you, Daniel. Thank you for forgiving me and helping me find what I lost."

The two girls spent several hours together. They laughed, shared stories, and became friends.

*****

After Maria entered Samantha's room, she found the girl on her bed, trying to read a book. She watched for several moments and then spoke, "Samantha, I know it's late, but we need to talk."

Samantha glanced over at Maria, then sat up. "What's wrong?" she asked.

Maria moved over and sat next to Samantha. "Daniel mentioned leaving on the morning train," she said.

Samantha started, surprised at the information. "What? Why?"

"Because she's smart enough to see something both you and Jenifer have missed," Maria stated. Then quietly she added, "And so am I."

Samantha looked down and fiddled with the quilt that covered her bed. "I know. Jenifer and I fought about it on the way home."

Maria nodded. "I thought you might have." She then proceeded to tell Samantha what she and Daniel had discussed.

"She said if one happens, so doesn't the other." Maria concluded, "If we allow Jenifer to drive a wedge between the three of us, then there will also be a wedge between the two of you."

Samantha nodded. "But Jenifer is so angry. And I must admit that I am too."

"Everyone was," Maria responded, "angry and hurt. But we have to work together to overcome those feelings." She sighed. "Samantha, you and Jenifer were like sisters. Surely, you're not going to let this little argument destroy that. If you do, then what hope is there for us?"

With that thought, Maria left, leaving Samantha to think on her words.

The night that followed was a long one. All the girls tossed and turned, thinking about the talks that had gone on.

Morning came early the next day. Samantha quietly dressed and headed downstairs to the parlor. Since dawn had just broken, she was surprised to hear voices.

She hurried into the parlor and stopped suddenly, surprised at the sight before her. Jenifer and Daniel were sitting there, studying a map of the world.

Samantha smiled when she heard the awe in Daniel's voice as Jenifer explained the places she planned to travel to once she had graduated. She couldn't help but laugh when she heard her sister say "perhaps you'll come back out West someday and see our part of the world again."

Her laugh drew the attention of the two girls. Their smiles faded however as they saw Samantha standing there.

Jenifer stepped forward. "Samantha, I think we need to talk."

The talk only took fifteen minutes, and by the end of it, the two girls were hugging and weeping.

As the Stones came down for breakfast, they were shocked to see all four girls sitting together and laughing like they were old friends.

"I take back what I said before," Mrs. Stone said with a smile. "I'm glad those girls came to Boston."

Mr. Stone smiled down at his wife. "So am I, Celia. So am I."

The morning passed quickly, and soon, one o'clock had arrived. The group was sitting in the parlor when Ella entered.

"I'm sorry to interrupt," the servant girl said. "But there is a boy here. He said that Miss Samantha invited him."

Samantha rose to her feet. "It must be James. I met him at the play last night and invited him to go sightseeing with us."

She left the parlor and returned a moment later with a boy following behind her. "Everyone, this is James," she introduced.

Once everyone had formally met, the five teenagers headed outside.

"It's a lovely day for a walk," Maria stated. "Why don't we leave the carriage?"

The others agreed, and they started toward town. When they reached the memorial gardens, they sat down to take a rest.

"What would you girls like to do first?" James asked.

The four girls looked at one another.

"What about a riverboat ride?" Samantha suggested.

The others agreed, and they started for the docks.

Ten minutes later, they were boarding the boat.

"The Charles River is about eight miles long," James stated as they found their places.

"The route we're following takes us by Old North Church. History records it as being the one from which Paul Revere had his friends signal to let the patriot riders know how the British planned to travel."

The girls listened to his historical lecture. Each found the information fascinating.

The ride started out smoothly, and they all enjoyed the experience. Unfortunately, Daniel soon discovered that the ride did not agree with her. Jenifer found her in a corner of the stern, sitting with her head on her knees and looking pale.

"Are you alright?" she asked.

Daniel shook her head.

"I'm sorry. I didn't realize the ride would make you ill."

Daniel smiled slightly. "Neither did I." She laid her heard back down with a groan. "Don't let me stop you from enjoying the ride. I'll be fine once we're on land again."

Jenifer smiled at Daniel. "Don't worry," she said. "I'm sure it won't be long now." She started to rise, but a large wave suddenly rocked the boat. She stumbled and suddenly found herself falling. She let out a scream just as she hit the water.

Samantha was standing on the bow of the boat when she heard a scream. She had been standing with James, talking with him as he pointed out the interesting sights they passed.

A pair of turtles had just slipped beneath the water when suddenly the current picked up. It rocked the boat roughly, and Samantha stumbled against James.

Placing a hand on her arm to steady her, James looked down at Samantha. "I've enjoyed our time together," he said sincerely. "I wish we had more of it."

Samantha had found herself nodding. "I do too," she said. Then she quickly added, "But surely you must realize that nothing could come of it. You have your school here, and I am going back out West with my sisters."

James had captured her other hand and held them both as he looked directly at her. "I hope that doesn't mean we can't remain friends," he said seriously. Then a bit more shyly he continued, "Would it be alright if I write to you?"

Samantha had smiled. "Only if I can write back," she had replied. That was when she had heard the scream.

Glancing up, Samantha saw a person dive over the side of the boat. Before she could fully comprehend what was going on, she saw Maria rushing to the railing. Samantha had heard her sister cry "Daniel, no!"

Rushing to stand beside her sister, Samantha saw two people in the water. One was Daniel, the other Jenifer.

She watched as Daniel struggled to keep both herself and Jenifer above the water. On her own, Daniel would have had no problem, but Jenifer's heavy skirts were threatening to drag her under.

Looking around, Samantha suddenly realized why the water had become so rough. They were close to where the Charles River met with Mystic River and Chelsea Creek before entering Boston's Main Channel.

"James, do something!" Samantha cried as the two girls in the water disappeared. Before they could do anything however, the girls reappeared, and Daniel managed to drag them over to the boat.

James and another male passenger reached down to help Jenifer into the boat. As soon as she was safely aboard, they reached back down for Daniel. But the boat shifted and struck the girl, and she disappeared from view.

"No!" Both Samantha and Maria cried at the same time.

The captain of the boat held his craft steady as the passengers looked for any sign of the girl. But she never reappeared. After thirty minutes, everyone knew all hope was gone, and the boat continued its way to Boston Harbor.

As James delivered the girls home, clouds moved in, and the spring rains fell upon Boston. The minute they entered, Mr. and Mrs. Stone realized something was wrong.

Realizing the girls were too upset to explain, James spoke up, "We were on the Charles River, and Jenifer was knocked overboard. Daniel dove in to save her, but she…she didn't make it."

Mrs. Stone gasped. "Oh my," she whispered. "Those poor girls." Regaining her composure, she turned to James. "Would you mind going to the hotel and getting Mr. Thompson? He is Maria's legal guardian and takes care of the girls."

James nodded and quickly disappeared. Twenty minutes later, he was back, and Mr. Thompson was with him.

Immediately he went to Maria and embraced the sobbing girl. "It'll be alright, Maria," he said, attempting to comfort her. "It will be alright."

CHAPTER 10
Going Home

The young girl on the riverbank came to slowly. As she stared up at the sky above her, a few drops of rain splattered against her cheek.

Dazed, the girl sat up and raised a hand to her temple. She was surprised when it came away red and sticky. Shakily she got to her feet.

Looking around, she saw she was in a harbor. Slowly she started making her way to a dock that stood in the distance. As she stumbled up to the pier, she caught sight of an old fisherman.

Stumbling up to him, she said, "Please…sir…help me…" Then she fell into his arms.

The old fisherman, and retired sailor, was caught completely by surprise. Looking down at the small girl in his arms, he lifted her and took her to his home, which stood on the wharf.

"Anna!" he shouted.

His wife appeared instantly. "Ira? What are you doing home so early?" She froze when she saw the girl in his arms. "Who is this?" she asked.

Ira looked down at the girl and said, "She stumbled up to me on the docks. She seems hurt." His voice was gruff, but his tone was tender.

Anna quickly ushered him into their bedroom. "Lay her down," she ordered. When he had done so, she said, "Now get me some clean water and a rag."

Once her husband had brought her the supplies, Anna began to care for the gash on the girl's temple. "This looks serious, Ira. I think you'd best get the doctor."

"No," a quiet voice said.

The elderly couple turned back to the girl on the bed.

"No doctor…please…" she whispered.

Anna moved over to sit next to the girl. "You've got a serious cut on your head—" she began, but Daniel interrupted her.

"No doctor…sisters…must think I'm…I'm dead. Staying at the…at the Stone Mansion." That was all she managed before she slipped back into unconsciousness.

"Did she say she had sisters?" Ira questioned. "One's staying at the Stone Mansion?"

His wife nodded. "I think you'd better go after them."

"Anna, they wouldn't even let me in the front door," Ira protested. "Folks like them don't talk to folks like us."

"Then you go to the back door! And you talk until you're blue in the face," Anna snapped.

Taking a breath, she calmed herself and said, "Ira, that little girl has a family out there—one that thinks she's dead from the sounds of it. We've got to get her back to them."

Ira sighed. "What if I can't find them? If she's been gone long enough that they think she's dead, they might have moved on."

Anna shot to her feet, her old eyes snapping. "Ira Fredricks, you get to that house and see about finding those girls. Or you can just go sleep on the docks with the fish."

After fifty years of marriage, Ira had learned it was best to do what his wife wanted when she was this angry. With a few mumbles, he headed back out into the rainy weather.

When he was gone, Anna turned back to the girl. "You poor child," she said softly. "If Ira can't find your family, we'll take care of you."

Ira made his way through the rain and wind. As a fisherman, he mostly kept to the docks, but he managed to work his way through the city.

Due to the weather, very few people were out. However, just when he was about to give up and head back home, he spotted a man making his way through the storm.

"Hey there!" Ira called. His voice carried above the wind.

The man turned, and Ira hurried to him. "I'm looking for the Stone Mansion, mate. Can you tell me how to get there?"

"I was just heading there myself. You can walk along with me," the man replied. "Miss Stone was involved in a boating mishap. I've been asked to come and see to her."

It was then that Ira noticed the medical bag in the man's hand. "I hope it's nothing too serious," he said, a little less gruffly.

The doctor shook his head. "I don't believe so. But I was told that she went underwater for quite some time."

Soon, they reached the mansion, and the doctor knocked on the door. They were admitted by a servant girl and led to the parlor.

Mr. and Mrs. Stone were sitting in the parlor with two young girls. All four looked up as the newcomers approached. "Thank you for coming, Doctor, especially in this weather," Celia Stone said, rising.

The doctor smiled. "It is my duty, Mrs. Stone." He then turned to the two girls. "I am sorry for your loss, my dears," he said kindly. Then he followed Mrs. Stone upstairs.

Ira shuffled his feet and cleared his throat, reminding everyone of his presence. Mr. Stone turned to him. "How can I help you, sir?" he asked.

Again, Ira shifted and said, "I'm not sure how to say this, Mr. Stone, but I've come to talk to these two lasses."

Mr. Stone cast a sideways look at Samantha and Maria. Their expression clearly showed that they had no clue as to who the man was.

"I'm sorry, sir, but the girls just experienced a terrible loss—" Mr. Stone began, but he was interrupted.

"Dash it all, man!" Ira exploded. "Would you let an old man say what he come to say before booting him out into this gale?"

He looked at the two girls, who had risen to their feet, startled by the outburst. "I'm sorry. I didn't mean to scare you girls. It's just an old man's temper. I didn't mean no harm." He took a breath and then said, "I was fishing on the docks this evening." He paused. "That's how I make my living, you see," he interjected. "And a small lass came up and begged me for help. Then she dropped like an anchor, and I barely managed to catch her to keep her from falling."

Realizing he was rambling, he coughed and then said, "I took her home so my wife Anna could tend to her. The lass was hurt, you see, and when she come too, she mentioned something about sisters. She was afraid they thought she was dead. Well, the lass said they were staying here and begged us to find them."

After he had awkwardly concluded his tale, silence filled the room. It was soon broken by the doctor and Mrs. Stone coming down the main stairs.

"I assure you, Mrs. Stone, that it is nothing serious. She has no signs of water in her lungs. Still, I would watch her, just to be sure."

Celia was about to thank the doctor when they entered the room and froze. "Paul, is something wrong?" Celia asked her husband.

Mr. Stone turned to his wife. "Mister..." He paused. "I'm sorry, I didn't catch your name, sir."

Ira quickly introduced himself, and Paul began again. "Mr. Fredricks says that Daniel is alive and is at his house on the docks. His wife Anna is taking care of her."

Before anyone could say anything else, Samantha rose. "Mr. Fredricks, would you please take us to Daniel?"

"I think not, missy," Ira responded. "Not until this storm has passed."

The girls protested, but Mrs. Stone said, "Mr. Fredricks is right, girls. It won't help your sister if something should happen to you."

"My Anna will take right good care of the lass." Ira tried to assure the girls. "I can swear to that."

Turning to Mr. Stone, Ira said, "If it's alright with you, mate, I'll come back after the storm 'as passed. Then I can take the girls to their sister."

"Of course, Mr. Thompson and I shall accompany them," Mr. Stone said, motioning to the foreman.

Ira nodded. "I figured you would. The docks can be a rough place at times."

Suddenly the doctor cleared his throat. "You said the girl was hurt. Perhaps I should come with you now."

Ira shook his head. "I don't think that'd be a good idea. The girl, well, she didn't like the idea of being checked out by a doctor. Seemed plumb terrified of the idea. My Anna will care for her until things get sorted out."

Another awkward silence fell over the group. Finally, Mr. Stone said, "Mr. Fredricks, why don't you stay here for the night?"

Ira shook his head. "No, I ought to be getting back. Anna might need some help." A few minutes later, Ira headed back out into the storm and headed for the docks.

When he opened the door to his house, Anna came out to meet him. "Did you find them?" she asked.

Ira nodded. "Yes, they'll come once the storm stops." He moved over to the stove to warm himself. Then he asked, "How is the lass?"

Anna cast a motherly glance toward the bedroom. "She's resting." Then she said, "I've made some supper. Once we've eaten, I'll take some into her."

When they finished and Anna was taking some food to the girl, she was surprised to see Daniel leaning against the wall. "What do you think you are doing?" Anna asked, setting the plate on the side table.

Startled, Daniel jerked her head up and nearly lost her balance. "My…my sisters…I've got to find my sisters…"

Gently Anna placed her hands on the small girl's shoulders. "You need to rest and eat something." Once she got her back on the bed, Anna said, "Ira found your sisters. They know you're alive and will come for you once the storm stops."

Relief flooded the girl's expression.

Anna smiled and handed her the plate she had prepared. "Eat that, then try to rest." She watched as the girl ate, then decided to ask, "What happened, Daniel?"

The girl looked up sharply.

"Your sisters mentioned your name to Ira," Anna told the girl.

Daniel shrugged and returned her attention to the meal. "I got hit with a boat," she said. Then she told the events that had brought her there. She finished by saying, "I'm sorry to be so much trouble."

Anna shook her head and took the plate from Daniel's hands. "It was no trouble, my dear. I'm glad we were able to help you."

The storm continued for three more days. During that time, Daniel grew close to the Fredrickses. She enjoyed listening to Ira's tales of the sea as the two sat mending finishing nets. She often shared a story of her own.

But even as they got to know one another, the Fredrickses could tell that something was bothering the girl. They decided to let it be, thinking that she might tell them when she was ready.

On her second night at the Fredrickses', Daniel insisted she move to the cot the couple had set up. "I won't put you out any more than I already have," she insisted.

It was the morning of her third day there when the storm finally broke. Daniel became restless, waiting for her sisters to arrive, and finally, Ira invited her to go fishing with him.

That was where Samantha and Maria found them several hours later.

As the two girls left the carriage, they spotted Ira sitting on the edge of the dock. Next to him, a girl sat, staring at the sea beyond. Immediately the two sisters ran toward them.

At the sound of running footsteps, Daniel turned. She jumped to her feet and ran to meet them. She stopped, however, when they were still a few yards away and turned from them.

Surprised, Samantha and Maria slowed to a walk as they approached her. They were even more surprised to see their younger sister shaking.

"Daniel?" Maria asked. "What's wrong?"

Daniel refused to look at her.

Samantha grasped Daniel's shoulder and forced the girl to look up at her. She was surprised to see tears in her sister's eyes. "It's alright, Daniel. Everything's going to be alright now. We're all safe and—"

Daniel cut her off. "But we're not," she said, pulling away from Samantha. Turning away from them, she gripped the dock's railing tightly. "Did they…did they ever find Jenifer?"

Samantha's eyes widened in shock. She felt a chill run through her as she realized that her sister didn't know. Daniel didn't know that Jenifer had made it back aboard safely.

The girl must think that Jenifer had drowned in the river. She must also believe that Samantha was angry—angry that Daniel had made it but had failed to save her best friend.

The shock dulled to disbelief, and Samantha finally managed to stammer, "Daniel…Jenifer's alright too. You got her back onto the boat before…before you disappeared. She wanted to come here but…but Aunt Celia wouldn't let her."

This time, when Samantha reached out and pulled her, Daniel went willingly into her embrace. To her surprise, Daniel let the older girl hold her and stroke her long hair soothingly.

Finally, the younger girl spoke. "When I first came to," she said, "my first thought was of you and Maria. Then when Captain Fredricks said you were coming, I got scared. I thought…" Finally, Daniel looked up at her sister. "Can we go home now?" she asked quietly.

Samantha hugged her tighter and said, "Yes, Daniel. If Mr. Thompson has finished his business, we can go home now."

ABOUT THE AUTHOR

Young Cherokee author Elizabeth Jean Thomas was born in Northeast Oklahoma. Some of her fondest memories of growing up include spending time with her family. This includes her parents, a twin brother, and three older sisters. Despite the sixteen-year age gap between the twins and the youngest of the older sisters, the three were always close. They spent a lot of time together, and many of their adventures inspired events which occur in Elizabeth's stories.

One of her favorite childhood memories is of growing up being read to. Elizabeth believes this is what instilled her love of reading and her dream to become a writer. As she grew, that love and dream grew stronger. Being homeschooled until she graduated high school was an encouragement in this area.

When Elizabeth was five years old, she gave her life to Christ. When she turned eight, she was baptized. Since then, Elizabeth has strived to follow God's will for her life. Part of that will was moving with her family to Central Illinois, where she remained for six years before returning to Oklahoma.

To this day, Elizabeth still enjoys reading the words of others, and she still loves writing stories of her own. In 2023, she began to publish her first book, *The Locket's Secret*. She hopes to publish many more.